ASBO

-A Novel of Extreme Terror-

by Iain Rob Wright

ASBO

A Novel of Extreme Horror

ISBN-13: 978-1470165260
ISBN-10: 1470165260

Cover art by Stephen Bryant

Interior design by Iain Rob Wright

www.iainrobwright.co.uk

Give feedback on the book at:
iain.robert.wright@hotmail.co.uk

Twitter: @iainrobwright

Second Edition

Printed in the U.S.A

Anti-Social Behaviour Order (ASBO): issued in response to "conduct which caused or was likely to cause harm, harassment, alarm, or distress, to one or more persons not of the same household as him or herself and where an ASBO is seen as necessary to protect relevant persons from further anti-social acts by the Defendant.

It is the failing of youth not to be able to restrain its own violence.
- Lucius Annaeus Seneca

Violence isn't always evil. What's evil is the infatuation with violence.
- Jim Morrison

-1-

"Those trouble-makers are hanging around outside again. Must be ten of them now. Should we call the police?"

Andrew turned to his wife, Penelope. She was peeking out of the living room window through a gap in the curtains. "They're just harmless kids," he told her. "We were young too, once upon a time. Not that I can remember that far back anymore."

Pen dragged herself away from the curtain and allowed herself to crack a smile. It was a rarity these days, which made the gesture all the more attractive. "You're thirty-eight, Andrew," she told him, inflecting her words with a sarcastic tone. "I don't think your memory is going just yet."

"Exactly, and I can remember being a sixteen-year-old with nothing to do. Me and my brother used to get up to all kinds of mischief. Didn't mean we were out to hurt anyone. Just ignore them and they'll ignore you."

"Isn't that what they say about wasps?" Pen spoke without turning around, too busy resuming her spying through the curtains. She'd been doing it now, on and off, for the last ten minutes and didn't seem able to pry herself away. Outside, the streetlamps had turned on with the arrival of dusk and were casting angular shadows over her face. She looked like a private detective out of one of those old Film Noirs.

Andrew couldn't help but giggle. "Wasps, snakes, rabid dogs, whatever. I think it makes pretty good sense in most situations. In other words, stop being such a nosey parker."

Pen let go of the curtain and let it sweep back into place. She padded towards him, barefoot, across the beige carpet of the living room and let out a deep sigh. "I know, I know. They just make me uncomfortable. Where've they come from all a sudden? Why do they have to be right outside my house?"

Andrew wrapped his arms around his wife, enjoying the warm feeling of her hips through her blouse. The flesh there was softer now than it had been ten years ago when they'd married, but still trim for a woman of forty. Pen worked the rowing machine every Wednesday and Friday and it showed. Andrew was a lucky man. He kissed her forehead.

"I think you mean our house," he told her. "Anyway, will you just stop worrying? The kids outside haven't done anything wrong, have they?"

Pen shook her head against his chest. "You're right, I'm just being silly."

"Don't worry, I'm used to it. Now what's for dinner, woman?"

Pen slapped him on the arm with a stinging backhand. "You'll get put to bed on an empty stomach if you call me woman again, cheeky sod."

"Did I hear someone mention dinner?"

Andrew spotted his daughter coming down the stairs in nothing but a plump white towel. Her shoulder-length brown hair was a wet and tangled mess around her glistening shoulders.

Andrew sighed. "You're not a little girl anymore, Bex. I really wish you wouldn't walk around half-naked."

She rolled her eyes. "I just got out the shower. Anyway, back to my earlier question: did I hear someone mention dinner?"

"Sit down, sweetheart." Pen dumped herself down on the room's bulbous, cream sofa and patted the cushion beside her. "Let me get those knots out of your hair. You look like something out of a horror movie."

Bex walked across the living room with her arms outstretched like a badly acted mummy. Then she collapsed on the sofa like a make-believe bullet had hit her in the forehead. Finally, she sat still long enough for her mother to run her fingers through the tangled bunches of her hair. She winced every time a knot was yanked.

Andrew glanced at his fourteen-year old daughter's naked legs and wished once more that she would cover them up. She doesn't realise how much of a woman she's becoming. Time she started being a little more aware of herself.

Bex caught his stares and frowned at him, pulling down the hem of the towel so that it was closer to her knees. She knew him well enough by now to recognise his looks of disapproval. She raised her eyebrows at him. "Can we have chippy?"

Andrew looked at Pen for approval, not particularly fussed himself. He wasn't a big eater most nights.

Pen shrugged her shoulders. "I don't mind chips."

Bex clapped her hands excitedly. "Cod and chips, please, Dad. Salt, no vinegar."

Andrew laughed. "Don't you think I know that? Been feeding you fourteen bloody years."

"And if you don't feed me again soon, I might not make it to fifteen." Becky sucked in her cheeks so that she looked like a starving ghoul. Add the chaotic mess of her hair and the impression was quite convincing.

Andrew let out his breath in a whistle. "Alright, drama queen, I'll get going right away; don't want you to starve. I'm going to walk, though – save the petrol – but then the three of us can settle down and watch a movie together. Isn't there a Stephen King film on tonight, Bex?"

"Yeah," she replied eagerly, pulling away from her mother's hair-straightening fingers and flopping back on the sofa. Her hair was now sufficiently straightened to pass for human. "Don't think it's for you, though, Dad; has monsters and stuff. You don't like blood and violence."

"Perhaps I'll make an exception if it means spending some time with my increasingly-absent daughter. You never have any time for me anymore."

"It's because you smell so bad."

"Charming. I suppose you're too good for a bit of BO now that you're a teenager.

Pen interrupted the exchange. "Can we save the banter for after we've all eaten? You're as bad as she is sometimes, Andrew."

Andrew put his hands up in defence. "I'm going."

He left the warmth of the living room and stepped into the chillier hallway, heading to his right. His shoes were in the front porch and he went to retrieve them, whistling a made-up tune as he went. He saw the group of youths through the glass window of the PVC front door. Pen had been right: there were about ten of them in total, mostly boys – but not all. Andrew counted at least two young girls about Rebecca's age.

He still stood by what he had said earlier: they were just bored kids with nothing better to do. It wasn't like there was a cinema to go to, or a bowling alley. In fact there wasn't anything for the kids to do in town during the evenings. They needed to venture into Birmingham for anything beyond a scrappy game of football. The kids outside were just trying to entertain themselves. No reason to be frightened of them. In fact, it would likely make things worse. If you treated young people like thugs all the time then that's probably how they'd end up behaving.

Kick a dog and it'll bite.

Andrew pushed aside his shoes and decided on a pair of trainers instead. The Nike running shoes were new and a little uncomfortable, but he wanted to try and wear them in quickly. He tied the laces loosely to reduce the pinching on his toes, then stood up and pulled his brown leather wallet from his jeans to check he had cash. He did – just over twenty-pounds in notes and change. The final thing he did was pull on his long, black overcoat from the stand in the corner. Even from inside the porch, it was clear that the weather outside was nippy. A tough winter was on its way.

Andrew fastened the final button on his jacket and was ready to leave. He unlocked the front door and stepped out into the bitter, grey dusk of the evening. The frosty air immediately gravitated towards him and he gave his shoulders a quick, yet vigorous rub as he started down the pathway. The dozen-or-so teenagers across the road noticed Andrew's presence as he left his property, but they paid him hardly any attention. Just like he'd told Pen, there was nothing to worry about. In fact, he was going to walk right by them on his way to the shops. He was willing to bet that they wouldn't make so much as a peep at him.

"Oi, mate?"

Andrew stopped in his tracks and frowned. Obviously he was wrong. No matter.

"Oi, mate, you fuckin' deaf?"

Andrew turned to the youths, who were a few feet down the road. Sets of gleaming eyeballs stared back at him, scrutinising him from beneath the glow of the streetlights. He cleared his throat and tried to speak calmly. "Excuse me?"

One of the youths stepped away from the others: a tightly-muscled teenager in a red woollen hat pulled low over his forehead. The lad had a thin scar across his lower lip and seemed to twitch periodically.

"Got a cigarette, mate?" the lad asked, twitching.

"I'm afraid I don't smoke," Andrew replied honestly.

The lad just stared at him, almost as if he recognised Andrew somehow, so was the spark of familiarity glinting in his eyes. It wasn't possible though. Andrew had never set eyes on the boy before.

"I said I don't smoke. I don't have a cigarette to give you."

The lad continued staring. His nervous twitch seemed to have increased its intensity.

"Okay then," he eventually said. "No worries."

Andrew resumed his journey towards the shops. See, no problem at all. A slight lack of manners, admittedly, but no worse than that.

"Get us some fags from the shop then."

Andrew stopped again and wondered if he'd just heard correctly. He took in a deep breath and let it out slowly, thinking what to say in reply to such an audacious demand. It was probably best not let it get to him and to just remain courteous.

"Okay," Andrew said. "I'm on my way to the shops anyway. You want to give me the money now or when I get back?"

The whole gang laughed like a pack of hyenas, but the twitching teenager in the red woollen hat did not find anything amusing. He marched forward, closing in enough that he was almost nose-to-nose with Andrew. The stench of stale beer permeated the young man's every breath as he spoke. "Don't think you understand, mate. You're going to buy me some fags because you like me."

Andrew took a step backwards, reclaiming some of his personal space. He attempted a laugh, but it came out as an asphyxiated splutter. "I-I... I don't think so, son. Get your own bloody cigarettes, okay?"

The teenager took another step forward and this time snarled right in Andrew's face. The stench of beer was nauseating. "Listen, cunt. If you get back from that shop without my fucking cigarettes, your head is going to hit this cement. You get me?"

Andrew tumbled backwards under what he could only describe as utter shock. Such threats and brutish behaviour were beyond his comprehension. He was furious. He was livid. That this wretched little thug felt he had any right to threaten him this way...

Yet, for some reason, all he did was walk away with his head down, his mouth closed. He heard the word 'prick' muttered by a female voice behind him, but he did not turn back. A numb kind of disbelief had washed over Andrew and the feeling in the pit of his stomach was like a white-hot poker thudding against his ribs.

It was a good five minutes before he regained control over his thoughts enough that he could begin to process what had just happened, but by that time he was already several hundred yards away from the gang and almost at the small row of shops that marked his destination. The chip shop was just up ahead.

He shook his head in disbelief. I can't believe that...that thug...spoke to me like that. How dare he threaten me! Who does he think he is? To think I was sticking up for those bloody kids not thirty minutes ago...

Andrew scratched at the stubble on his chin and hissed at the night. Pen had been right. They were all a bunch of troublemakers. He crossed the road and headed into the chip shop, determined not to let the nasty little exchange affect him a minute more than it already had. Inside was a member of staff he recognised – a young blond girl who'd served him several times before. They'd never spoken in a personal way but she always had a warm smile to greet him with. Tonight was no exception and he felt a little less angry as the girl showed her usual politeness by welcoming him in from the cold. Not all teenagers were bad.

He quickly placed his order for his and Penelope's food, as well as Bex's – salt, no vinegar – before standing aside and warming himself on the chip shop's hot metal counter. His entire body seemed to unload its weight onto his elbows as he leaned, like he'd been fighting off the urge to fall down this whole time without realising it. The amount of anger he felt was worrying, yet he felt strangely vacant at the same time. It was as if the encounter with the gang had sent him into some sort of daze.

He still had to walk back past them to get home.

What the hell should he do? He wasn't going to let them scare him into not walking the street outside his own home. He sighed and rubbed at his eyes. He should have said something – stood up to them. They were probably a bunch of cowards faced with a responsible adult. If they were still there on the way back, Andrew decided he was going to say something. He couldn't let this stand.

"-ful they're hot."

Andrew looked up from the counter. "Huh?"

The blond girl nodded to a plastic bag in front of him. "I said, careful they're hot."

Andrew took the bag full of food and thanked her, then paid her. He wandered towards the door, but before he got there, the girl called after him.

"Are you okay?"

Andrew turned back around, wondering what it was about him that had caused the girl concern. Was it so obvious that he was rattled?

"I'm fine," he said. "Just had a run in with a gang of youths. Haven't quite calmed down about it yet."

The girl's face dropped. "You don't mean Frankie Walker, do you?"

Andrew shrugged. "Don't know their names."

"Red beanie hat? Has a twitch?"

Andrew nodded.

The girl shook her head and wore a grim expression. "I'd be careful if I were you. He just got out of a young offender's home and he's been messed up ever since – in fact he was pretty messed up before."

Andrew huffed. "He's just a boy. I'm not going to let him intimidate me."

"Just watch yourself, okay? I mean it. He's a nasty piece of work."

Andrew stood in the doorway and thought for a moment. It felt wrong to let a teenaged boy frighten him. This was a country where everyone had the right to be free, safe, and happy. No one had the right to take those things away from him. He wouldn't allow it.

"What's your name?" Andrew asked the girl behind the counter.

"Charlie."

"Well, Charlie," he did his best to smile, "thanks for the advice, but I think I'll be just fine. You take care, okay?" He pulled open the door and stepped back out into the cold. The night had arrived fully since he'd been inside the chip shop and the world had gone dark beyond the streetlights that lit the small shopping area with their narrow cones of light.

As he started his walk down the road, the warming aroma of hot chips and acrid vinegar made his mouth water, and suddenly he couldn't wait to get home. It was a greasy, unhealthy dinner, but he could stand to put a few pounds on his slender frame anyway. A bit of junk food never hurt anybody. He picked up speed, hunger encouraging him onwards. Rounding the final corner before home, he thought about the youths again. It was surprising that his mind had briefly turned to other things, but it'd been easier once he'd decided that this Frankie and his followers were not going to intimidate him. Despite that, it was a relief when it turned out the group of youths had gone, moved on from their previous spot. The corner was free of their presence and the cones of light from the streetlights illuminated nothing now but the cracked and worn pavement of the road.

The cowards didn't have the courage to stay and go through with their threats.

Andrew was just about to smile with satisfaction when he heard voices. He strained his eyes, seeking out bodies in the darkness, but ended up having to use his ears to hone in on the appropriate direction. The noise was coming from several yards ahead.

The youths were loitering around a Mercedes sat on the curb in front of Andrew's house – it was his Mercedes. Frankie was sat on the bonnet, leaning back on his elbows and laughing loudly.

"Cretin!" Andrew almost spat the word as he headed across the street.

Frankie saw him coming and waved happily.

Andrew gritted his teeth. Don't you wave at me, you insolent little shit.

"Hey, mate," Frankie said, his eyes narrowed beneath the brow of his beanie hat. "You got my cigarettes?"

Andrew rushed over to the group and this time felt none of the shock or anxiety that had plagued him during his earlier encounter. This time he was angry. "No, I haven't got your goddamn cigarettes! Get the hell off my car."

Frankie did as he was told. He slid off the bright red bonnet of Andrew's car and then looked back behind him, admiring the vehicle. "Nice motor, mate. What is it, an SLK, yeah?"

"Yes," said Andrew. Impatience now enveloped every word that came out of his mouth. "Just step away from it, please. It's brand new."

Frankie nodded his head and whistled. "You hear that everyone? Brand new Mercedes. Nice."

"Yeah," said a young girl beside him. Her unkind face was caked in gaudy make-up and framed by streaky-blonde hair. Her breasts were practically hanging out of her top despite the chilly weather. "Thinks he's well bling, innit," she said, "with his flash motor."

Andrew stared at the girl and shook his head. "Do you know how stupid you sound, young lady?"

"Thinks his shit don't stink," added a Black youth, identical to the lad standing next to him. They were obviously twins, matching in both genetics and clothing – they wore the exact same blue jeans and non-descript white t-shirts.

"I don't think anything like that," said Andrew. "I just think you should respect other people's property, and that pretty young girls should be home this time of night."

Andrew didn't know why he used the word 'pretty', as she was anything but. It was meant only as a placating gesture to try and stem the animosity. It seemed to do the opposite, though, and the girl scowled and spat right at him.

"Fucking Perv," she said. "You're a pedo, innit? A kiddie-fiddler!"

Andrew's temper broke its bonds. "How dare you. Show some bloody respect to your elders, you spiteful brat."

Frankie shot forward and shoved Andrew in the shoulder, jarring the plastic bag from his hand and spilling the chips all over the road. Then he poked Andrew hard in the chest, repeating the stabbing gesture with each word that came out of his mouth. "I... think... you... need... to... respect... me..."

The sudden fright flooded Andrew's system with adrenaline and his stomach turned over so violently that he was almost sick over the teenager's shoes.

But he wasn't going to allow himself to be intimidated by this hooligan again. No way in hell.

Andrew snarled. "Why the hell would I respect an idiot like you? You're nothing but a pathetic bully trying to show off in front of his friends."

Frankie seemed to enjoy Andrew's reaction. He turned and looked over his shoulder at his cronies. They were all laughing and their loose circle tightened around what they no doubt considered to be light entertainment.

"Now, now," said Frankie in a voice so patronising it sounded like he was trying to talk to a child. "No need to get upset, mate. We're just talking. In fact, it's me what should be upset."

Andrew huffed. "Why, exactly, is that?"

Frankie punched Andrew in the stomach. The sudden pain was excruciating and took away his breath so completely that it felt like he no longer had lungs. He fell to his knees, clutching at the air desperately for help.

Frankie crouched down beside him and whispered in his ear. "I asked you for a pack of cigarettes and you just mugged me off – not to mention perving at my girlfriend. I thought we understood each other, mate, but you hurt my feelings."

Andrew couldn't speak. The tightness in his chest and stomach seemed like it would never let up, like he'd never manage to take another breath again. Mortal panic took control of every cell in his body as he struggled to suck in even the tiniest morsel of oxygen.

Frankie straightened up and kissed his boney fist like a trophy. Then he chuckled. "Come on, gangsters," he said to his giggling cronies. "Let's leave this piece of shit to eat his chips up off the floor. We'll carry this on another day. Nice trainers by the way, mate. Got to get me a pair of those."

Andrew rolled onto his side and groaned as the youths left him. Gradually – very gradually – his breath came back to him in great heaving gasps. Part of him wished for his family to run out and comfort him, but another part – a bigger part – made the thought of them seeing him like this intolerable. He tried to get to his feet, using his palms against the floor to steady him. He was shaken and sick, but his stomach just about managed to control itself. When he looked down at the scattered chips and mashed-up cod on the floor Andrew realised he was crying. Several lonely tears crept down his cheeks and left freezing-cold trails behind them. He didn't know if they'd been caused by pain and fear, or shame and humiliation. The fact that someone had frightened him to such a point made him pathetic. The fact that it was a child made him feel even more worthless.

He shot forward and heaved up the meagre contents of his near-empty stomach, coating the discarded chips on the floor in a hot broth of undigested coffee and biscuits he'd eaten earlier. Three minutes later, he wiped his mouth and started the long, lonely journey up the path to his house. It no longer felt like home.

-2-

Andrew sank down onto the bench in his porch and took some deep breaths – each one was painful. He kicked off his trainers and just sat there a while. He'd already hung up his coat and was ready to go inside, but for some reason he just couldn't. Once he'd sat down it was impossible to get back up. Something held him in place, as though his very presence inside the house would infect his family with something terrible.

Maybe he was just too ashamed to face them?

But I can't stay here all night.

No one had come out during the attack and that could only mean Pen and Bex hadn't witnessed what'd happened. It was a major relief, but still didn't change the fact that Andrew had just been assaulted.

What the hell should he do? Call the police?

His mind was a muddle. He couldn't think straight. In a lot of ways he'd not yet fully accepted reality to the point of resolution. The answers were still murky and unclear. For now, he decided to will himself back to his feet and go back inside the house. He wouldn't find any answers alone inside the porch.

He stepped through into the hallway where Pen was coming down the stairs. She wore her fluffy pink dressing gown and was rubbing at her hair with a towel. Obviously she'd decided to fit in a quick shower while he'd gone to get the chips.

Damn it! The chips... What did he say?

"Hi, hun," Pen said, smiling. "You okay?"

Andrew nodded. "Fine."

"Where's the food?"

"It's...well it's..."

Penelope stepped up to him and placed a hand against his cheek. "Andrew, what's wrong?"

"Nothing," he answered quickly. "Bloody chip shop had a problem with their fryers and had to close early. Wasted journey."

"That's okay," she said soothingly, probably knowing something was up with him. "We'll just order Chinese."

"Sounds good." Andrew felt like breaking down in her arms and sobbing, but he didn't.

"Honey, has something happened?"

Andrew shook his head and pushed her away. "I've just got a stomachache coming on. Think I'll have a bath and go to bed. You and Bex eat without me, okay?"

Pen frowned at him. "You said you'd watch a film with her."

Andrew started up the stairs. "Sorry for getting ill. I'll try not to be so fucking inconsiderate next time."

There was no reply behind him and Andrew knew it was because his wife was shocked. Swearing was not his style at all.

He closed his eyes and chided himself. I shouldn't take things out on her. She's just concerned about me.

Hell, I'm concerned about me.

He reached the top of the stairs and turned left towards the bathroom, where he opened the door and stepped inside, pulling the plastic dolphin on the light-cord. The bulb flickered on and hurt his eyes with its harsh glare reflecting off the white walltiles. Somehow the pain in his retinas seemed to reactivate the pain in his abdomen and he doubled over. He dropped down to his knees and leant over the bathtub, reaching across and turning on both taps at once. He listened to the soothing gush of fresh water for a few seconds, then slipped the plug into the drain and let the tub fill up.

When it was halfway full, Andrew stood up and peeled off his shirt. He caught a glimpse of himself in the full-length mirror fixed to the back of the bathroom door and hissed. A deep, grey blemish of a developing bruise bloomed beneath the ribs on his right side. Gently, he ran a finger over the injury and pressed down slightly. The action was immediately met with a sharp, stabbing pain that radiated through his entire torso. His stomach fluttered with approaching nausea and forced him to lean over the sink and take deep breaths. It took several minutes before his insides calmed down again.

Hands shaking, he unfastened his jeans and let them fall around his ankles, his underwear too. Then he stepped out of the clothes and pulled off his socks using his toes, unable to bend down and pull them off by hand. Once he was completely naked, he stepped over into the bath and gingerly lowered himself down. The warm water sent fresh stabs of pain through his ribs, but after a few seconds the agony subsided and was even alleviated slightly as the therapeutic heat massaged his body. He slid back and placed his head down on the spongy bath pillow that Pen had bought needlessly on one of her extravagant shopping trips. He was grateful for it now, though, and the softness against the back of his skull made him feel sleepy.

He would have to make up with Pen before he went to bed – apologise to her. Never going to bed on an argument was a wisdom he'd always abided by. Whether or not he shared the reasons why he had snapped in the first place was something he had not yet decided.

Didn't want to worry her.

But didn't want to keep things from her either.

Andrew used the toes on his left foot to turn off the hot water tap followed by the cold. He slid lower into the water, letting his chin touch the surface. If he could have, he would have gone completely under, accepting the warm and inviting embrace of the water like a protective womb, but he settled for dunking his head under briefly and soaking his hair. Wet, brown strands plastered his forehead when he came back up and he wiped them away with his hand. Relaxation approached at last, the tension flowing away into the bath water. Soon Andrew would be able to think things through rationally – to decide whether or not he would call the police, tell his wife, or just keep the whole thing to himself. With a calmer mind, he could at least console himself that things would work out one-way or another. He was a middle-classed citizen of the UK, not some impoverished Russian on the mean streets of Moscow. There was order and civility in England. Wretched little monsters like Frankie were punished for their crimes.

A knock at the bathroom's door.

"Andrew?" It was Pen.

Andrew sighed, wishing that the water would swallow him whole. He still wasn't ready to speak to his wife. But what choice did he have?

"Andrew, I ordered you some food as well. Just in case you change your mind. I'm worried about you. Is your stomachache really bad?"

"Yeah," Andrew replied. "But I'll try to eat something anyway. I'm sorry I shouted at you."

There was a brief pause, but then an answer. "That's okay. We all get grouchy when we're not very well."

Andrew suddenly felt teary. His wife's compassion was such a contrast to the animosity of earlier events that it sent his brain into an emotional tailspin, but he fought back the tears and made himself smile. "I love you, Pen."

"I love you too, hun. I'll see you downstairs, okay? That film is about to start and Rebecca wants you to watch it with her."

"Okay. Be right down."

Andrew leant forward in the bath and winced against the stiffness and pain that bloomed in his ribs. He yanked the chain attached to the plug and listened to the gurgle as the drain began its suction. Then he lay back down and waited for the water to drain away around him, enjoying the sensual tickle of the water level dropping against his skin. When the tub was finally empty, he remained there for several more minutes, not wanting to move or face the chill of the air outside his ceramic cocoon.

When he did finally find the willpower to get out of the bath, Andrew quickly grabbed a towel from the warming rail and wrapped it tight around himself. There was a hidden breeze in the room that nipped at his shoulder blades in places the towel did not cover. He fought back a shiver and began to dry himself, taking care not to be too rough around his sore ribs. Not wanting to add needlessly to the washing pile, he gathered his clothes off the bathroom floor and decided to put them back on again. The jeans were comfortable and would be fine for sitting and watching a film. Perhaps he would get into pyjamas later, after dinner.

The plush carpet of the landing outside the bathroom felt good beneath his feet as he padded back towards the stairs and started down them. As he neared the bottom, he could hear the loud blaring of the television from the living room. For some reason, his daughter was unable to enjoy anything that didn't carry the risk of hearing damage.

Andrew reached the downstairs hallway and was just about to enter the living room...

A knock at the door.

The Chinese is here. Andrew changed direction and headed for the porch instead. He stepped inside and tried to make out the figure behind the glass door, but it was too dark outside, so he opened the door.

There was no one there.

Andrew stared out into the darkness, straining his eyes for shapes in the shadows. All of the light was behind him, making the darkness in front of him deep and unending. He leant forward and focused his eye, but still he could see no one. He started to think for a moment that he'd just imagined the knock at the door.

"Alright, mate?"

Andrew jumped back as a figure appeared from behind the sidewall of the porch on the left and entered the bleeding patch of light from the hallway. It was Frankie.

Andrew's eyes narrowed. "What the hell do you want?"

"Chill out," Frankie replied, face twitching and scarred mouth grinning. "No need to shit your pants. I came to apologise, innit."

Andrew's eyes narrowed further. "What?"

Frankie moved forward and placed a foot onto the step of the front door. Andrew moved forward to meet him.

"I said, I've come to apologise," Frankie lifted the brow of his red beanie hat in a way that was almost gentlemanly, "about tonight's earlier...misunderstanding."

Andrew laughed. "You mean when you assaulted me for no good reason?"

Frankie laughed back. "Yeah, I guess you could put it like that. No reason we can't be friends though. You and me, we can be bros."

"We'll never be friends," said Andrew, "and I already have a brother, so get the hell off my property and clear off."

Frankie's smile left his face and his twitch seemed to get worse for a moment. "Careful, mate. I don't appreciate being told what to do, you get me?"

Andrew shook his head. "Look, what do you want? I've done nothing to you."

"I know," Frankie agreed. "Which is why I'm going to allow you to make peace."

"Make peace? I didn't do anything to breach the peace."

Frankie sighed. "You going to fuckin' listen to me, mate, or am I going to have to drop you again?"

"How dare you threaten me in my own home."

"Fuck your home. This whole neighbourhood is mine. You want to be left alone; you do what I tell you. Give me your trainers."

Andrew was taken aback. “Sorry?”

“Give me them sweet-ass Nikes and you’ll be left alone.”

“Go away, you monster.”

Frankie grabbed Andrew around the throat and sneered. Andrew struggled back and managed to escape the grip, but his heart was now racing.

“Do you want to die?” Frankie asked coldly.

Andrew shook his head in disbelief. “You’re insane.”

“I’ll cut you up and snort your remains if I feel like it. Question is: are you going to behave and do as you’re told, or do I have to show you your own blood?”

Andrew went to reply but was interrupted.

“Who’s at the door, Andrew?” It was Pen shouting from the living room.

Frankie smirked, tried to move inside the porch.

“N-No one,” said Andrew, forcing Frankie back. “I’ll just be a minute.”

“I thought maybe it was the Chinese.”

“No, I’ll...I’ll let you know when it’s here.”

Frankie was still smirking. “Going to have a nice dinner with the missus? You go off the idea of chips then?” He pushed forward again, half-inside the doorway now. “Maybe I should join you? Say, don’t you have a fine ass daughter I’ve seen around here?”

Andrew pushed the youth back out of the door. “You leave my family the fuck alone.”

Frankie said nothing, just continued smirking, not leaving.

“What do you want?”

“I already told you.”

Andrew swallowed a lump in his throat, tried to maintain eye contact with Frankie, but failed. He sighed, picked up the Nike trainers from the shoe rack, and threw them out of the door. “Here! Now leave me alone, you vulture.”

Frankie sniggered. “You think I’m going to pick ‘em up off the floor? Go get ‘em and hand ‘em to me properly.”

“Are you serious?”

Frankie glared.

Andrew threw his hands up in the air. “Fine! It would be my goddamn pleasure.” He stepped outside and gathered up the shoes from the pavement. Then he returned to Frankie and thrust the trainers into the teenager’s arms. “Now leave me alone.”

“Deal’s a deal, mate. Have a nice life.” He walked away just as another figure came up the path, holding up a brown paper bag.

"Chinese delivery, sir?"

Andrew took the bag from the deliveryman and tried to smile, but found it impossible, so he just paid for the food and gave a good tip. The last thing he felt right now was hungry. In fact he felt downright sick.

-3-

Getting to sleep was a long and lonely struggle. Pen had started her gentle snoring as soon as her head hit the pillow, but Andrew lay next to her for what seemed like hours, staring up at the ceiling, his head swirling with unwanted thoughts.

The movie Bex had made him watch was disturbing, full of monsters and giant insects feasting off the flesh of the living. The ending had been bleak and depressing, but Bex seemed to enjoy it, grinning between mouthfuls of noodles and chicken.

The film wasn't what was kept Andrew awake though. Frankie haunted his mind like a relentless boogieman. Every time sleep came, the boy's scarred and twitching face would jar Andrew back awake. It was now 4:00AM.

Three hours till work.

Andrew's job as an Ad Exec wasn't physically taxing, but it did require a great deal of concentration and focus. The project he was working on at the moment for a Soda company was especially important – the rebranding of a nationally recognised product. The stress of last night's events was a concern he could do without right now.

He took a deep breath and closed his eyes. If there were any chance of him getting an iota of sleep, he would need to clear his mind. He needed to forget that he'd let an adolescent bully him and take his trainers. It was done and he should forget it, but the humiliation weighed down on him so heavily that it felt as if his skull may split open on the pillow and spill out his cowardice.

4:40AM.

The minutes flew by and Andrew's mind flittered between numb consciousness and troubled sleep. His waking thoughts were so vivid that they merged with his dreams to the point that he had no idea whether he was asleep or awake.

5:01AM

Noise.

From downstairs.

Andrew's eyes snapped open. He was pretty sure the noises had been real, that he had been awake to hear them and not imagining things in his sleep. It had sounded like a door opening.

5:13AM.

Another sound.

Somehow Andrew had snoozed another ten minutes, the beckoning embrace of sleep managing to override his grasp on reality, but now he was awake fully.

Footsteps.

Someone was inside the house.

There was another sound, closer, but he quickly realised that it was Pen snoring. The noises downstairs, however, were less explainable.

Someone was inside the house. Or was it Bex?

Andrew summoned the courage to get out of bed. Chinese food worked its way up his gullet. His legs wobbled as he set them down on the soft carpet. The sounds downstairs had stopped, but he was sure that there had been a break in. Bex would not be wandering around at this time in the morning. His mouth filled with saliva and he had to swallow several times as he exited the bedroom into the unlit landing. Bex's door was open as usual, and he looked inside. His daughter was asleep, snoring softly in the identical way that her mother did, tucked up beneath her plush duvet. It wasn't her making the noises.

Andrew reached the end of the hallway and looked down the stairs, cocking his head to listen for more sounds. He could detect nothing and a slither of hope suggested he'd imagined it all; that the scary movie – and his altercation with Frankie – had spooked his anxious mind.

He pressed the switch at the bottom of the stairs and blinked as the light filled his adjusting eyes. The downstairs hallway was clear, untouched. The photos on the wall were still in place and his grandmother's bureau was undisturbed. So far so good.

He moved over to the living room door and paused outside of it. This was the room with the television, Blu Ray player, and other things worth stealing. If anything were missing, it would likely be from this room.

And if anybody was still inside, they were most likely inside in this room.

Andrew took a deep breath and pushed open the door, clutching the handle tightly as he turned it. A smell hit him as he entered the darkness – a bitter, salty odour, along with something else that was more acrid.

Vinegar?

Andrew reached along the wall and found the light switch, familiar enough with his own home to find it in the dark. His finger lingered over the switch for a moment as his stomach performed somersaults. As much as he needed to see the state of his living room, he also wanted to delay things for as long as possible. Once the lights were on, he would be forced to deal with the situation. Right now, he was safe in the dark and oblivious.

Couldn't put things off forever, though.

He switched on the light.

The room came into view in a flash, and at first presented too much visual information for his brain to interpret all at once. One thing, however, slowly became clear. There was nothing missing.

Thank god.

But a few moments later it also became clear that something had been added. All over the room was a mulched-up mess of what looked like...

Fish and chips.

A cod had been stamped into the carpet, while dozens of loose chips had been mashed against the sofa's upholstery. Even the walls were smeared in deep-fried potato. The smell of salt and vinegar enveloped the room, pungent to the point of making Andrew's eyes water. It wasn't long before he put two and two together – that he realised the fish and chips were a message from the person responsible for knocking them out of his hands several hours before.

Frankie had done this.

***

The police arrived within the hour, just as the sun rose. The light coming through the window bathed the living room in an orange ambience that seemed unsuitable in the presence of such mess. Pen and Bex sat, huddled together, on the sofa in their nightgowns. Andrew sat at the dining room table with the two police officers – a straight-faced man and an amiable blonde woman, PC Wardsley and PC Dalton.

"What time did you hear the noises, Mr ...?"

"Goodman. Andrew Goodman. And I don't know exactly, but it was around 5AM, I think."

"Okay," said the female police officer, PC Dalton, whilst PC Wardsley took notes. "What exactly did you hear?"

Andrew felt like he was going to have a breakdown, so exhausted from lack of sleep. He did his best to answer calmly, though. "I'm pretty sure that I heard doors opening and closing and somebody creeping around."

"Did it sound like just one person?"

Andrew nodded. "I suppose so."

Dalton smiled warmly, performing the gestures she'd doubtlessly learned through sensitivity training. "Do you have any ideas how someone could have entered your home, Mr Goodman? Were all the doors locked?"

Andrew shrugged and looked down at the table, not wanting to make eye contact with the female officer. "I don't know," he admitted. "Before tonight, I never really worried about locking everything up at night. It's a nice neighbourhood. The front and back doors were locked, of course, but I may have left a window open."

"We won't be doing that again," Pen added tersely from the sofa, before returning to the dazed silence she'd displayed since waking to this mess.

"No," said Andrew. "We won't."

PC Dalton asked her next question. "Do you know anyone who would want to do this to you? Nothing was taken, so it seems causing upset was the main motive for the break in."

Andrew listened to the sound of his own breathing for a few seconds, wishing the whole thing would just go away. But it wasn't going to, was it, no matter how much he wanted it to. So he gave his answer: "Frankie."

The male police officer, Wardsley, raised an eyebrow then and looked surprised. "Frankie?"

Andrew nodded. "There's a gang been hanging around the last few days. I think their leader is a lad named Frankie?"

Wardsley scribbled down some notes eagerly, whilst his partner, Dalton, resumed questioning. "Why do you think this Frankie would want to target you?"

Andrew glanced over at his wife and daughter. Both were now looking at him with great interest. He turned back to the female officer and sighed. "I know, because the bastard assaulted me yesterday evening – punched me in the stomach. I was carrying fish and chips at the time and they spilled all over the road."

"What?" Penelope shouted. "Why on earth did you not tell me? You sat with us all night and you didn't think to tell us that you'd been attacked?"

Andrew looked at her and felt shame. Bex started to cry, which only made the feeling worse. "I'm sorry," he told them both honestly. "I didn't want to worry you."

Pen folded her arms and shook her head at him. "Worry me? What do you think all this is doing?"

"Okay," Dalton said, sliding a strand of blonde hair behind her ear. "Can you describe this man, Andrew?"

"Teenager," Andrew corrected. "Barely past being a kid."

"Okay. What else?"

"He's muscly – like he works out a lot. Red beanie hat. Has a scar across his lip and a weird facial tic thing."

"He has a twitch?"

"Yeah," Andrew confirmed.

"Anything else?"

"The girl who served me at the chip shop said Frankie had just gotten out of a kid's prison, and that he's a complete psycho."

"God," Pen uttered, covering her mouth with her hand. "How did you get mixed up in all this, Andrew?"

He felt a pinch of aggression, but managed to keep his anger emerging. "I didn't have much choice, Pen. I had to walk past him on the way to the chip shop. Apparently that's all it takes to wind this guy up."

"None of this is your fault, sir," Dalton said firmly, glancing at Pen as she spoke. "I'm afraid this is just the way some of today's youth get their kicks."

"So what do we do?" asked Bex, sounding frightened. "How do we get this Frankie to leave us alone?"

"I take it you're going to arrest him?" Pen asked the officers.

"We will question him, see what he has to say."

"What?" Andrew couldn't believe it. "That's it? You'll go have a chat with him? He'll deny everything."

"We will see what the forensic team brings up when they search the house a little later," the man, Wardsley said. "If we find Frankie's prints then we will arrest him. Did anyone see him assault you last night?"

Andrew shook his head.

Wardsley stood up and patted Andrew on the back. "Okay, let me make a call to see what I can find out about this Frankie. In the meantime pop the kettle on to calm your nerves. Things can all seem very overwhelming at this point."

"Okay." Andrew nodded. "Thank you.

Dalton got up and went after her partner. They both went outside and returned to their squad car parked outside on the curb.

Andrew joined his family on the sofa.

"I can't believe this has happened," Pen told him. "That bastard was in my home."

Andrew put an arm around her. "It'll be okay. The police will do something about it."

"Ha! You heard them, they probably won't be able to do anything."

Andrew sighed. "Look, let's just see what happens. No need to assume the worst yet."

"Are you okay, Dad?" Bex asked. "Did you get hurt when they attacked you?"

"What do you think?" Pen snapped at her. "There's nothing pleasant about being assaulted, is there?"

Andrew hushed his wife. "Calm down. It's not Rebecca's fault. I'm fine, Bex, thank you. Just some sore ribs, but I'll live. I'll take today off work and rest up."

Pen shook her head at him angrily, yet the tears in her eyes betrayed the upset that she was really feeling. "Don't you ever keep something like that from me again, Andrew."

"Yeah, never," Bex added.

Andrew reached over so he could hug them both at the same time. "I promise. I'm sorry I didn't tell you before. What's done is done though. You should go to work as normal, Pen. Don't worry about me"

Pen nodded then looked at Bex. "I'll give you a lift to school, hun."

Bex frowned. "I don't even get to have the day off school? Sucks!"

Before any argument broke out on the subject, the police officers re-entered the room. Dalton was smiling politely, but Andrew could tell by her weary eyes that she didn't have good news for them.

"Mr Goodman," she said. "Would you like to step outside for a moment?"

"Why?"

"Because we have information that you may wish to share with your family separately."

Andrew didn't like the sound of that at all. He stood up and moved away from the sofa, following the officers out into the hallway. "What is it?" he asked, once they were out of earshot of his family.

Wardsley looked down at his notepad and began reciting what he had written. "We weren't personally aware of this individual when you first mentioned him, but then PC Dalton and I have recently exchanged from the Stratford branch. As it turns out, however, this Frankie is well known to the local branch."

"Who the hell is he?"

"A scumbag," replied Dalton, bluntly. "We shouldn't comment on such things, but Francis Walker was put in a young offender's institute at fifteen after stamping a fellow school pupil into a coma. When the police caught up to him, he had a grand's worth of cocaine on his person."

Andrew couldn't believe it. "What the hell was a kid doing with all that coke on him?"

Wardsley shrugged. "Most likely he was selling it for a supplier. It's common practise to get kids selling it – less suspicious. He obviously fell in with criminals at an early age and he's only gotten worse since being released."

"So why the hell is he back on the streets?"

"Because he was convicted as a child," said Dalton. "The courts take sympathy in such cases."

Andrew shook his head. "He should still be locked up. He's a thug."

Wardsley cleared his throat. "Frankie Walker may well have been misled as an innocent child, but that doesn't change the fact that since an early age all he has been exposed to is crime and violence. There's nothing else he knows and it's doubtful he'll ever reform. I agree with you, Mr Goodman."

"So get him off the street."

"We intend to do that, but I'm afraid we can only do so with sufficient evidence."

"Well, what do I do until then? How do I protect my family?"

Dalton handed him a contact card. "By locking up safe and calling us if anything else happens. We'll be here, okay?"

"We suggest keeping a diary," said Wardsley, "of any further incidents. You could also install CCTV cameras."

"Cameras? A diary? Are you kidding me?"

Wardsley shrugged. "May sound silly, but it will help support any cases we bring against Frankie in the future."

Andrew put a hand against his forehead. It was clammy. "I can't believe this. It's just a bunch of kids. Am I really in danger here?"

"Probably not," said PC Wardsley, "but Frankie is an unsavoury individual. It won't hurt to be over-cautious. Take care and call us if anything happens. Anything at all."

Andrew let the police officers out of the house, locking the porch door behind them. He watched them drive off and the whole time he was thinking: an unsavoury individual...

Just how unsavoury are we talking?

-4-

Davie Walker awoke on an unfamiliar couch in an unfamiliar house. His back ached from his neck all the way down to his tailbone, and it took several, confused minutes before he could remember where he was. There had been a party.

How much did he drink last night? He felt like a lorry parked on his head.

Several other people lay sprawled across the room, all semi-conscience and moaning in the same hungover way that he was. Crumpled beer cans and empty bottles of vodka littered the floor, making it look more like a landfill than a home.

It must have been one hell of a party.

Davie rolled off of the sofa onto his knees. The carpet was wet beneath him, soaked with alcohol – or vomit. He felt it seep unpleasantly through to his jeans. Rising to his feet, he took a couple of unsteady footsteps, his vision struggling to focus as he moved across the lounge. A half-naked girl lay sprawled in his path, uncovered breasts pointing at the ceiling like beacons. Davie stepped over her like a speed bump and pushed through the door in front of him.

It led into a kitchen that was as much a chaotic mess as the lounge had been; only this time pizza and discarded snack food littered the floor in addition to all the beer cans. There was only one other person in the room – Dominic –passed out on the breakfast bar with his legs hanging off the edge. It was strange to see Dom without his twin, Jordan, but then Davie noticed him lying beneath the breakfast bar, as paralytic as his brother.

Davie wondered where his own brother was. Frankie had disappeared around3AM, but had promised to make it back to the party before daylight. Davie hoped he was okay and just shacked up with some bird – not seeking out trouble like he'd been doing non-stop since he'd got out the nick two months ago.

Davie left the twins sleeping and exited into the next room. If his fuzzy memory of last night served him correctly, he would find a staircase that would hopefully lead him to a bathroom. If he didn't piss soon, he was going to burst.

Sure enough, Davie found himself in a beige-carpeted hallway with a staircase. He hurried up the steps two at a time, his bladder almost releasing itself as it anticipated imminent release. The bathroom was on the left. He pushed the door open urgently and dashed for the toilet. The bowl was already full of bright-yellow piss but Davie was happy to add to it, sighing orgasmically as his bladder expelled its bitter contents.

It was then that he heard shuffling beside him.

Davie turned his head, still peeing too heavily to turn around fully. The noises seemed to be coming from the bathtub, from behind the shower curtain. There was someone there. He was powerless not to finish urinating, so that's what he did first. Once he was finished, he hastily pulled the shower curtain aside.

The boy in the bathtub was bound and gagged, secured to the unit's mixer tap by a series of linked-up cable-ties. A gym sock filled his mouth and that, too, was secured by a cable tie pulled sadistically tight around his head. Completing the boy's restraints were several more cable ties around his ankles. The boy looked weary – like he'd been there all night.

Davie reached into his pocket and pulled out his knife. The boy's eyes widened with fear, but it wasn't his intention to harm him. He slid the blade beneath the cable tie around the boy's face and began sawing back and forth.

Eventually, the cable tie snapped free.

"You're all fucking crazy," the boy shouted after spitting out the sock.

"Calm down," said Davie. "Who the hell are you, anyway?"

"Who the hell am I? This is my house you're in."

Davie found that surprising. "So what are you doing tied up in here then?"

"Because some psychopath crashed my birthday party and beat me up."

It was then that Davie noticed the bruising around the boy's face. Someone had given him a birthday to remember. "Who beat you up?"

"I did," said Frankie, entering the room behind him. "I told him to chill out but he insisted on calling the police. Had to put him down."

The boy shook his head. There was fear in his eyes at the sight of Frankie. "You forced your way into my home. What did you expect I would do?"

Frankie perched himself on the edge of the bathtub and looked down at the boy. "Me and my mates were just looking to party. We could have all been friends, but you had to be selfish and keep all the fun to yourself."

"You're a monster. You won't get away with this."

"We should go," Davie told his brother. "Last thing we need is any more trouble. You only just got out."

Frankie put a hand on Davie's shoulder. There was a strong smell coming off his hands – like vinegar. "You worry too much, little bro," he said.

"And you worry too little."

"Okay, okay, fuck me." Frankie raised his hands up in front of his face and adjusted his beanie hat. "Just let me take a piss first, okay?"

Davie nodded and stepped away from the toilet. Frankie stood in front of it and undid the buttons on his flies, popping them free one by one. Davie turned around to give him some privacy, but quickly turned back when he heard screams from the bathtub.

Frankie had moved away from the toilet and was now urinating all over the cable-tied boy, causing him to struggle and choke as the golden stream covered his face and mouth.

Davie stood in the doorway, stunned. "Shit, Frankie, what are you doing?"

Frankie laughed heartily. "Hey, when a man's got to go, a man's got to go."

"Just stop it. He's already going to call the pigs, so stop making things worse."

Frankie finished pissing and turned to face his brother. "You're right, Davie. You're always right. I should probably help the poor guy get cleaned up. Make things better for myself."

Davie was suspicious. Frankie wasn't prone to sudden bouts of compassion. At least not since he got out of prison.

Frankie winked at Davie and turned back around. He reached up for the chrome shower taps that were set into the tiled wall above the bathtub and gave one of them a hearty twist. Water cascaded from the showerhead, soaking the boy held captive below. Davie watched him squirm, a little at first, but then more urgently. Eventually the squirms turned to full-blown thrashing and Davie realised why.

Frankie had turned on the hot tap.

As the water heated up, the boy began to wail. His face turned red as the cable ties held him powerless beneath the scolding embrace. Davie moved forward to help, but Frankie shouldered him out of the room, pulling the door closed behind them as they stood on the landing.

"Leave it," said Frankie. "Quit acting like a pussy."

Davie sighed. "You just got out of the nick. You'll end up straight back there if you keep pulling this bullshit all the time. First you rob that guy's trainers last night and now you're burning people's faces. It's messed up."

Frankie shot out his arm, shoving his smaller brother up against the wall. "I'll decide what's fucked up. Who feeds you, Davie? That's right, I fuckin' do. If you have a problem with how I roll, then you can piss off. I've looked after you long enough to deserve a little respect."

Frankie stormed off down the corridor and headed downstairs. Davie listened to the boy in the bathtub, still screaming, and stepped inside to help him. Frankie was his brother and Davie loved him. He would always have his back, no matter what...

But this is getting out of hand.

Davie turned off the hot tap and looked down at the quivering boy in the bathtub. His face would never be the same again. Davie wondered how many more people would be damaged before his brother was through.

***

Davie caught up with Frankie outside. He had joined up with the twins, Dom and Jordan, and the three of them were sat waiting for him on a small brick wall outside the house.

"About time," said Frankie. "What were you doing in there?"

Davie shrugged. "Not in a rush, are you?"

"Never in a rush, me. The world is my oyster."

Davie covered the distance between him and his older brother and took a deep breath. The fresh air of approaching winter was invigorating and chased away the fringes of his hangover.

"That kid's really hurt," he said. "You're going to go straight back inside for this."

Frankie spat on the floor. "I ain't ever going back inside. I'll die first."

"Then what the hell are you playing at, pulling shit like this? Kid you burned is going to go straight to the pigs."

Frankie laughed, apparently unbothered. "No way, little bro. You want me to tell you why that little pissant is going to keep his mouth shut?"

Davie shrugged.

"Going to keep his mouth shut for two reasons. Number one: I've already made sure I have a dozen people ready to swear-down that I weren't nowhere near this house when the kid got burned. Number two: Dom and Jordan are about to go back inside and tell the kid that if he says one word to the pigs about me, they'll visit him in the middle of the night and cut his face off."

Davie rubbed at his forehead. "Fuck man. This is so messed up."

"Stop being such a whiny little pussy," said Dom.

Frankie turned around and pointed a finger in the twin's face. "Don't be talking shit to Davie. That's my blood, man. You get me?"

Dom nodded and stepped backwards as if to yield to Frankie's authority. Sometimes the respect his brother gained so easily from people left Davie in awe. It wasn't a skillset he himself possessed, or was ever likely to. Frankie was the strong one. Frankie was the one who people would always follow.

Even if it was straight to a prison cell.

Dom and Jordan went back inside to deliver their threat. Frankie pulled his brother aside and the two of them started walking. "You got to chill out, little bro," he said. "I know you're just trying to watch my back, but things are sound, man. I ain't going nowhere, you get me?"

Davie let out a sigh and kicked at a loose pebble on the ground. It hit the curb before scuttling into a drain. "I just want you to be careful. Things were hard while you were gone. You know, with mom and everything."

"Let the drunken bitch rot. I'm looking after you again now and this time it's for good. I learned a lot while I was banged up; stuff about how to keep the pigs off your back while bringing in the big dollar."

"By selling drugs."

Frankie stopped walking and looked at Davie. His expression was one of understanding and it reminded Davie of how kindhearted his brother used to be – when they were both much younger. It seemed like ages ago now.

"Yes, by selling drugs," said Frankie matter-of-factly. "You and I are going to live the good life. Get ourselves out of the shit we grew up with. I got it all covered, little bro."

"If you go down for dealin', you go down hard."

Frankie put his arm around Davie and pushed him back into walking. “Enough, man. Just chill out about it and leave the worrying to me. Got other things to be getting on with for now.”

“Like what?” asked Davie.

Frankie clapped his hands together and put on a big smile, stretching the scar across his lip. “We’re going to go and have ourselves some fun.”

Davie smiled back, but secretly his empty stomach was churning anxiously. Davie was beginning to not like his big brother’s idea of fun.

-5-

At twelve-o-clock Andrew entered the chip shop and looked for Charlie. To his relief, she was there, standing alone behind the counter as she had been the previous evening. As always, she smiled at him as he entered, but this time there was something a little apprehensive about her expression.

"Hey," Andrew said to her. "Working again?"

The girl nodded. "Need the money. Saving for my sister's hen party in Magaluf."

"Nice," said Andrew, thinking he couldn't imagine anywhere worse for a holiday.

"What can I get you?"

"Nothing actually. I'm here to see you."

Charlie looked worried, her mind perhaps jumping to conclusions.

Andrew put his hands up to reassure her that he wasn't after her number or anything else as inappropriate or weird. "I just wanted to ask you a question, that's all. Nothing big."

She relaxed a little, her shoulders lowering. "You want to ask about Frankie, don't you?"

Andrew nodded.

"He came in here last night, right before closing. Ordered fish and chips just like you did. I thought it was a coincidence."

"It wasn't," said Andrew.

Charlie leant forward on the counter and let out a sigh. "I really don't want to get involved. I told you to be careful."

Andrew stepped forward. "I know you did, because you're a nice, caring person. I need you to keep being that way, because this animal is endangering my family."

Charlie looked up from the counter and made eye contact with him. Her eyes were blue and seemed to shimmer with sadness. "What do you want to know?" she asked.

Andrew scratched at his head. "I don't know really. How do you know Frankie?"

"Went to school with him."

"And?"

Charlie shrugged. "And he was a nightmare. Beating other kids up, vandalising anything he could get his hands on, stealing, drinking, shagging. You name it and Frankie Walker did it. Eventually he went down for something or other. Assault I think."

"He just went to a young offender's home?"

"Yeah, he was only a kid at the time."

Andrew laughed. "That's all he is now. They should have kept him locked up."

"I agree."

"So what is he doing around here? I've never seen him before recently."

"He lives around here now," said Charlie.

Andrew shook his head. "No way. This is a nice area."

"Used to be. Council bought some of the property around here for social housing. Remember my dad kicking up a big fuss at the time. Got a petition going and everything."

Andrew leant forward onto the counter and let the weight off his legs. "I can't believe they would put someone like Frankie in a nice part of town."

"Where else should they put him? Keep the poor with the poor, right?"

Andrew straightened back up. "No...I don't know what I think at the moment. I guess I just thought all council houses were grouped together."

Charlie shrugged. "I think that's how it used to be. My dad said the Government wanted to space out council properties to avoid creating ghettos. That's the right word, yeah?"

Andrew nodded. "Yeah, ghetto is right. Except now it seems that we're all getting a little slice of ghetto to call our own."

The shop's door opened behind Andrew. Charlie wore her greeting smile as a customer walked in.

Guess everyone got the smile. Not just him.

"Look," said Charlie, leaning forwards. "Like I said, I don't want to get involved. But I can tell you that Frankie lives somewhere on Tanner's Avenue. I know because a girl who used to be my best friend is now a drugged-up skank, thanks to him. I haven't spoken to her in months, but that's where she used to go see him when we were still friends."

Andrew nodded and said thanks, but the girl was already serving the new customer, acting as though the conversation had never happened. Probably for the best, he thought as he left the shop and headed for home.

So Frankie has a home. Perhaps he has parents there? He's still just a kid, so someone should be in charge of him. Maybe someone that has a little bit of control over him.

Andrew didn't hold up much hope, but it was an option. Maybe Frankie would leave him alone if his own family knew of his behaviour. Andrew considered making the journey to Tanner's lane later this evening.

Maybe I can put a stop to this before anything else happens.

Andrew turned the corner and lost his breath at the sight that met him there. His bright red Mercedes had been modified. Its expensive bodywork was now emblazoned by coarse, black gloss-paint, spelling out words in several places.

The words read: pedo.

Pedo, Pedo, Pedo.

***

Andrew fell back into his armchair in the lounge and stared into space. The sounds of his family's voices were a distant droning, buzzing in the distance like irritated wasps. He was hearing their words but was unable to assemble them into cognitive meanings. Eventually he had to will his mind to return back to reality.

"...ell are they playing at?"

Andrew looked up at his wife, standing before him and shaking like a leaf. "Huh?"

"I said, what the hell are they playing at? Who behaves like this? Animals!"

Andrew leant his head back against the armchair's headrest and examined the ceiling. The wind in his lungs seemed to stick in his throat as he let out a breath. "I don't know. I just don't know. I still can't believe any of this has happened."

"Why you, though, dad?" Bex asked from the sofa. She was holding up well, but Andrew knew that deep down she was just as unnerved as her mother.

Andrew lowered his head and shrugged at his daughter. "Don't know sweetie.

If it wasn't me then it would have just been someone else."

"I still don't understand why you won't call the police again," said Pen.

"Because it won't do any good. Unless someone saw it happen, they will have nothing to go on."

Pen clicked her fingers at him and motioned for him to get up. "Well bloody well find out if anyone did see. Ask the neighbours."

Andrew took another moment to stare into space, before eventually nodding his head. "Okay. Maybe someone did see something."

Andrew stood up and left the room. He was already wearing his shoes – not something he usually did indoors but the carpet was already ruined with chip fat anyway – so he stepped through into the porch and opened the front door. Outside, his eyes again came to rest upon his vandalised vehicle and the disgusting words written all over it. There was no way he could drive to work until it was repainted. That led him to think what exactly he would say when he dropped it off at the garage.

Oh, I'm not a pedo. It's just some of the local kids having fun. Yeah right!

The street was deserted – the vandals come and gone without any remnant of their presence. It seemed unlikely that anyone had witnessed the crime. It was a Tuesday morning and Andrew knew that most of the people on his street had day jobs. The lack of parked cars only reinforced the assumption.

Next door, though – number 16 – was home to an elderly couple. Most likely they would be his best bet as they were both retired. The chance of them being home during the day was a healthy possibility. Andrew pressed their doorbell and waited.

It was a full minute later when he pressed the bell again.

Oh well. There goes my best shot.

He was just about to turn away when he noticed a twitch in the living room curtains. He couldn't be sure, but it seemed as though there had been someone looking out the window at him. Now they had slunk away, ignoring him.

"Hello," Andrew shouted, stepping back to try and get a better view of the window. The shifting silhouette confirmed to him that someone was indeed inside. "Excuse me," he said. "I need to talk to you, if that's okay?"

Nothing.

Andrew stood motionless, at a loss for what to do. Why wouldn't they talk to him? Why would a nice elderly couple that had said hello to him for years not want to open the door to him? When he turned around he realised the reason why: the words written on his car.

Pedo, pedo, pedo.

It was becoming clear that whatever happened from now on, no one was going to help him. The panic-inducing power of the words on his car was enough to turn his neighbours against him. Innocent or not, he would be seen as a deviant in their eyes. No smoke without fire.

They think I'm a paedophile.

***

Tanner's Avenue was a quiet cul-de-sac of terraced houses, lined on either side by leafless trees that towered above Andrew like judgemental skeletons. One of the homes belonged to Frankie, if what Charlie had told him was correct, but as for which one Andrew had no clue. There were at least twenty identical properties, each with the same drab lawns and featureless facades.

Andrew decided the best thing to do would be to just pick a house at random and ask the occupants if they knew which house was Frankie's. He chose a house with a green-painted door and a brass number plate: 17.

Upon knocking, it took about fifteen seconds for the door to be opened. A diminutive gentleman, at least in his early sixties, appeared in the doorway. His hair thinned above his delicate round spectacles and he seemed withered and stressed-out.

"Can I help you?" the man asked him in a tone that was in no way friendly.

"Hello there," said Andrew. "Sorry to bother you, but I was hoping you could tell me if you knew where a young man named Frankie lives."

The old man's eyes narrowed and he took a half step backwards.

"You know him?" asked Andrew.

"Who wants to know?"

"I do. He's been causing problems outside my house and I wanted to speak to his parents."

"Ha!" the man laughed so hard it sounded like something tore loose in his throat. "Good luck! There's only his mother to talk to and she's just as bad as him. Ruined this street that bloody family have. A plague on all our houses."

"The family?" asked Andrew. "The whole family is a problem?"

The man nodded. "That Frankie is an evil little bleeder, no argument about it, but you'll hardly blame him when you meet his degenerate mother. Never seen the woman sober the whole time she's lived here. Even passed out in the middle of the road once. Lucky someone didn't run her over...more's the pity."

Andrew shrugged his shoulders and already felt like the whole thing was a bad idea. It was the only option he had right now, though. "Can you point me to the right house pleae? I have to at least try to speak some sense to them."

The man sighed. "Like I said, good luck. They live at number 8."

Andrew thanked the man and moved away from his door. Number 8 was directly behind and he turned and made his way over to it. Reaching the house a moment later, he was surprised he hadn't realised sooner that it belonged to Frankie. The front door was chipped and dented, the paint peeling away in great chunks, whilst the path leading up to it was overgrown with weeds and discarded beer cans. One of the upper windows of the house was boarded-up while another was emblazoned with a faded England flag. If it were not for the bushes outside of the property, it would have stuck out like a sore thumb; a dilapidated slum amongst a row of far better kept properties.

Here goes nothing, Andrew told himself as he made his way up the path, having to step over what looked like a rotting condom on one of the slabs about half way up. There was no buzzer on the door – no knocker either – so he was forced to rap his knuckles against the sharp splinters of the rotting wood.

No one came to answer, but Andrew could hear commotion from somewhere inside of the house. It was the sound of someone clumsily making their way through the reception hallway, bumping into any nearby furniture en route. He held his breath and suddenly realised that his stomach was deeply unsettled. Having to wait so long for the door to open made the feeling even worse.

It was a full minute later when a dishevelled woman appeared. Her hair was wild on one side, but matted and damp on the other, as if she had been lying in a puddle.

"Wahya wan?" she asked.

Andrew smiled at the woman who, he now noticed, was wearing nothing but a flimsy nightgown that was a size too small. Her shinbones were covered in bruises. "Are you Frankie's mother?"

She gave Andrew a drilling stare. "Who are ya? Don't look like yer from the social."

"That's because I'm not."

"So wahya wan then?" The woman was shouting now, her words coming out in aggressive slurs and bad breath – alcohol and smoke. "Wahya wan with my Frankie?"

"So you are his mother? I was hoping you could have a word with him for me?"

"Talk to im about wah?"

Andrew took a deep breath and tried not to let the woman's inability to have a polite conversation deter him. He still believed that everyone had the capacity for rationality – it was just deeply buried in some people. Especially when they were drunk and possibly stoned.

"He's been causing me some problems," Andrew explained. "He broke into my home last night and today he vandalised my car."

The woman snorted back a nose full of snot. "Got proof?"

"Do I need it?" asked Andrew. "I'm simply asking you to talk to him. I don't wish to cause any trouble for you, ma'am. I just want Frankie to leave my family and me alone."

The woman huffed. "He don't listen to me, mate. Does wah he wans, that boy."

"But you're his mother."

"Don't mean a thing. Speak to im ya'self."

Before Andrew had a chance to stop her, the drunken woman was shouting up the stairs, yelling for Frankie to come down. Andrew felt his skin tighten as he anticipated another encounter with the young thug.

Frankie appeared behind his mother only a moment later, wearing nothing but a pair of black boxer shorts. She turned to look at him as he arrived. "Man says you been botherin' him."

Frankie looked at Andrew and his face lit up with recognition, but all he gave was a smirk. "Dunno what the bloke's on about. Never seen him before."

Frankie's mother shrugged her shoulders at Andrew. The motion made her nightdress ride inappropriately high. "Never seen ya in his life, he sez."

"With all due respect," said Andrew, "that's a lie."

Frankie pushed past his mother and stood in the doorway. "Who you calling a fuckin' liar?"

Andrew sighed. He wasn't going to get drawn into an argument. "Frankie, can we please just stop this? I have done nothing to you."

"I think you need a lie down, mate, cus I ain't got a clue what you're on about. Like I said, I ain't never seen you before."

Andrew clenched his fists, but then willed them to open again. Losing his cool would not help the situation. "Frankie, the police know all about you and what you've been doing. If you don't stop now you'll end up in trouble."

"I don't see how," said a young girl appearing in the doorway beside Frankie's mother, the same one who'd been with Frankie's group the night everything started – the one who had called Andrew a perv. She wore only a skimpy pair of pink shorts and a bra.

"He's been with me," she said. "Last couple of days we ain't left the bedroom, except to eat."

"See, yer wrong." Frankie's mother slurred at Andrew. "Want to watch who ya start accusin', mate."

"I am not wrong," Andrew stated firmly. "This young lady has been just as much involved in what's been going on as he has."

The girl laughed at him mockingly. "You must be stoned, mate. I would remember an old perv like you. You're talking a load of shit."

"You're Charlie's friend, aren't you?" Andrew said.

A spark of confusion flittered through the girl's eyes and, for a moment, her mocking contempt was completely diluted. A moment later it was back in full force. "Don't know a Charlie, mate. Who is he?"

Andrew finally lost his temper. "Look, you evil little shits. If you come near my family again, you'll regret it, okay? You've had your fun, but now it's time to move on. No more games."

Frankie leapt out of the doorway and shoved Andrew back along the path. "You think you can come down my manor and threaten me? You must be trippin'."

"Yeah," added Frankie's mother. "Get away from my house before I call the police."

"You'll call the police. That's bloody rich." Andrew was about to say more but realised it was pointless. He put his palms in the air and backed away. "Fine, have it your way, but this is going to stop one way or another."

"Just fuck off," Frankie shouted. "You come here again and you're a dead man."

Andrew sneered. "Same goes for you, my friend."

"He ain't your fuckin' friend," said the girl.

Andrew turned his back and walked away. He couldn't help wondering if he had just made things worse. The walk home was a long one.

-6-

Davie had watched Frankie's altercation from the top step. It wasn't the first time he'd seen his brother in a argument and it would no doubt not be the last. Their mother getting involved and making things worse wasn't particularly unusual either.

The man at the door had been middle-aged, older than the usual type of person Frankie had misdealings with. Davie assumed the man was the same one his brother had delivered a beat down to recently. Frankie hadn't mentioned it himself directly, but Dom and Jordan had been laughing about it at last night's party. The man had come to the door angry, but seemed more desperate than anything else – like he just wanted to call a truce.

Frankie was coming up the stairs now, casually, as if nothing had happened. Michelle was with him, both of them laughing.

"Hey," Davie said. "Who was that?"

"Fuck knows," said Frankie, "but the guy has a death wish to get all up in my face like he did."

Davie shook his head. "Don't shit me. Who was it?"

"Just some perv," answered Michelle. "Don't worry about it, D."

"My name is Davie. How did he know where we live?"

Frankie shrugged. Michelle answered again. "Stupid bitch, Charlie, must have told him. He knew we used to be friends so she obviously spoke to him at the chippy or summin'."

"Okay," said Davie, "so what did he want?"

"Fuck should I know?" said Frankie.

Davie looked at his brother and sighed. "I'm your brother, man. Tell me the truth."

After a couple seconds, Frankie finally relented and let his guard down, his demeanour softening. "Okay, little bro, you're right. He's just some geezer I had to teach a lesson in manners the other night. I gave him some grief and he just came round to kick off about it."

"So you're going to leave off now?"

Frankie laughed and patted Davie on the shoulder. "Hell no! Shit is only just getting started. Now get out my way. This bitch needs a good seeing to."

Michelle punched Frankie on the arm, but giggled as she did so. Davie got out of his brother's way without saying anything more. He wasn't in the mood to argue. Frankie would do as Frankie wanted; that was the way it had always been.

Davie decided to descend the stairs rather than return to his room. He entered the downstairs hallway on his way to the kitchen. It was unlikely there would be anything to eat – but stranger things had happened. The malodour of alcohol and weed was stronger downstairs than up and managed to permeate every corner of the house. The sound of daytime television polluted Davie's ears as much as the smell polluted his nose – the additional noise of Frankie and Michelle screwing loudly upstairs only added to the assault on his senses.

"Shouldn't you be at school?" his mother asked as tried to sneak past the living room.

"Half-term," he told her truthfully.

Davie's mother stared at him, trying to work out if he was lying or not. Davie stared right back at her. Eventually, she seemed satisfied. "Okay, sweetheart," she said. "Come sit with your old mom."

Davie smiled uncomfortably but joined his mother on the grimy settee as he was told. She pretty much lived in this room, sprawled in front of the television. Davie sometimes wondered whether her sweat-soaked flesh would someday fuse with the festering cloth of the cushions and keep her there forever.

His mother took a long swig of beer and followed it with a throaty belch. She looked at him. "So whaya bin up to, Davie?"

Davie shrugged and stared at the television. "Nothing really. Just hanging out with Frankie. I'm glad he's back."

His mother huffed and took another swig of beer. "Boy's a bad un. Done nothing but embarrass me his whole life. All I ever did was try to raise him like a good mother. You need to stay out of his way, Davie. You study hard and make your old mum proud. That boy will only bring you down with him – drinking, drugs, sex. He's no good."

"He's my brother. He just does what he needs to survive."

Davie's mother laughed a wet cackle that eventually became a hacking cough. Phlegm and spittle flew from between her cracked lips and settled on the grungy carpet. When she finally managed to get control of her lungs again, she said to him: "He tell ya that, did he? Bloody swine."

Davie didn't answer. He hated it when his mother started on about Frankie – it never ended well. There was a real, palpable hatred between the two of them. Davie was the unfortunate victim in the middle. He loved them both, but when it came right down to it, only one of them was really looking out for him – and it wasn't his mother.

The sounds of sex grew louder and more frenzied. Michelle cried out in orgasm, lacking regard for anyone forced to listen.

Davie's mother looked up at the ceiling and sneered. "Goddamn whore! Where does Frankie find 'em? Regret the day I gave birth to that monster, I really do."

"Mum, don't say that." Davie knew where things were going: same place they always did. "Just watch your TV show. Okay?"

Suddenly her demeanour changed. Her eyes turned dark and her expression exuded a deep and hateful bitterness. "Don't you tell me what to do, you ungrateful little shit. Who do you think you are?"

"Mum..."

Davie's mother struck him across the face. His instincts almost made him strike her right back, but he managed to refrain from any retaliation. You never hit women, Frankie always used to tell him, those are the rules. So instead, Davie stood up calmly to exit the room.

His mother shouted after him as he left. "That's right. Get outta my sight. Devil-child, that's what you are. You and your brother make my life a living hell." She started sobbing to herself. "What did I do to deserve this? I do my best..."

Davie ignored the rest of her comments, had heard them too often to let them settle in his mind. He turned away and went back up the stairs, heading for his bedroom. Maybe he would while away the day with a videogame or two. Before he got there, though, Frankie exited his own bedroom and stepped out onto the landing.

"What that bitch say to you?" he demanded. "I heard shouting."

"Nothing," said Davie. "She's just mouthing off at the television again. You know what she's like when she's been drinking."

Frankie examined Davie's face, trying to work him out. Eventually he nodded and said okay. "It's what she's like when she hasn't been drinking that I know nothing about. Woman's a waste of space." Frankie stepped over to Davie and put his hands on his shoulders. "Go find your coat, little bro. We're going out."

"Where to?"

Frankie smirked, his twitch turning the expression into an alternating grimace. "To go and have some fun."

Great, thought Davie, heading to fetch his coat. More fun...

-7-

Andrew was upset, frightened, angry, and a multitude of other unwanted states of emotion. The amount of adrenaline in his body had at one point almost driven him to full blown panic. It was only thanks to a combination of deep breathing and the brisk walk home that managed to keep his anxiety under control. Now that he was rounding the final corner to his house, his predominant emotion had become anger.

Frankie's attitude had been aggressive just like Andrew had expected it to be. What he had not expected was that the boy's mother would be just as confrontational as her son. In many ways, it explained a lot – almost made the monster that was Frankie understandable and perhaps even forgivable. It didn't make things right, though. Enough was enough.

Frankie was just a teenager, living with his mother and dating a school-girl. Andrew was willing to bet his watch that the lad was all front and little substance. He'd only had the guts to throw a punch at Andrew the previous night because of a gang backing him up. People were only afraid of Frankie because of the reputation he worked so hard to cultivate. Things would be different if people fought back instead of buying into it.

Andrew was an average-sized guy and man enough to throw a punch if he had to. If Frankie wanted to try and victimise him then he was welcome to try. Andrew knew where he lived now and who his family were. They were on an equal playing field.

He reached the path to his house and started walking up it. He could see the shape of Pen and Bex through the net curtains of the front window and smiled at the thought of seeing them. He didn't expect them both to be home yet.

Was it that time already?

Andrew checked his wristwatch and saw that it was getting on for six-o-clock. As if in affirmation of the late hour his stomach began to grumble. Food was something he hadn't thought about all day, but perhaps his appetite returning was a good sign – a sign that things were no longer getting to him quite so much.

Andrew unlocked his front door and stepped inside the porch. Then he kicked off his shoes, removed his jacket, and passed through into the hallway. Pen and Bex were on the sofa in the living room. The carpets were still a mess, but the smell was mostly gone now. They gawped at him as he entered.

"Where have you been?" Pen demanded. "Have you seen what they've done to your car?"

Andrew set himself down in his armchair and released a long, weary sigh. "I know. I went to that lad's home to try and put a stop to things."

Pen's eyes widened. "Really? What happened?"

Andrew leaned back into the chair's cushion and shrugged his shoulders. "Not a fat lot. The kid's whole family is as bad as he is. Was like banging my head against a brick wall."

"So this isn't over then?" Bex asked, sitting beside her mother and still wearing her school blazer.

Andrew shrugged again. "I'm hoping so, honey. The swine knows that I know where he lives now and that I'm not afraid to confront him. Hopefully that will be enough to make him think twice from now on. Either way, don't let it worry you. Things will be okay."

Bex seemed unconvinced. "How do you know?"

"I just do, okay? I'm not going to let anything bad happen."

"Okay," said Pen, finally sounding less on the defensive. "Let's just move on then." She looked at Andrew and grinned. "I think we're still owed an evening of fish and chips, so I think I'll walk over to the shops in a bit."

Andrew stood up from the armchair. "Don't be silly. I'll go."

"You sure?"

Andrew nodded emphatically. "Yes, of course. There's nothing to worry about. Last thing I thought you'd fancy though is fish and chips after last night."

"Like I said, we should just move on. Besides, I don't feel like cooking tonight.

You certain you don't want me to fetch them?"

Andrew nodded. "Certain as can be." He left the living room and went to get his jacket from the porch. It was chillier now as night fell, so he decided on a scarf also. Once he checked for his wallet and keys, he left the porch and started down the front path.

The sight of the empty road ahead was comforting, the soft buzzing of the streetlights the only sound he could hear. Right now, the memory of being attacked by a gang of bloody-minded yobos seemed impossible – a nightmare he had woken from long ago. Still, it would be smart to remain alert, and Andrew wasn't entirely confident as he ambled down the street. But at least for now it seemed like things would be okay and that events would soon blow over.

What a day. Just when life seems to be routine and unexciting, something crazy can happen and turn everything on its head. It's over now though. A little bit of grovelling at work and things will soon be back to normal.

Andrew didn't notice the ambulance at first. He became aware of the flashing lights at the edge of his vision, but was too lost in his own thoughts to recognise their immediate connotation. When he came to realise that someone was undoubtedly injured, Andrew hastened his steps and headed towards the gathering crowd.

The ambulance was parked outside the small group of local shops that Andrew had been heading for. When he realised that the emergency vehicle was parked directly outside of the chip shop, his stomach tied itself in knots. A bad feeling enveloped him like a shroud. He rushed forward and looked for the nearest paramedic. There was a young, blond man in a white shirt and green jacket. He was carrying a large holdall and NHS emblems adorned his clothing in several places. Andrew approached him.

"What's happened?" he asked. "Who's hurt?"

The paramedic pushed past him, not making eye contact. "Please move aside, sir."

Andrew went to grab out at the man's sleeve but missed. The medical worker hurried away before there was any opportunity for another try. Several spectators stood around in various corners of the shopping area and car park. Andrew examined them one after the other, eventually spotting a young girl wearing the same chip shop uniform that Charlie always wore. He sighed with relief.

"What happened?" Andrew asked the chip shop girl as he closed the distance between them.

The girl's eyes pointed at him and were moist with recently shed tears. It was obvious she'd witnessed whatever accident had befallen the poor soul in the ambulance.

Andrew put a hand on the girl's shoulder. "I said what happened?"

For a brief moment it looked like the girl was going to faint. Somehow she managed to refocus herself and look Andrew in the eye. "She...she got burned."

"Who got burned?"

"Cha...Charlie."

Andrew's knees threatened to fold beneath him. "Charlie is the one who got hurt?"

The grief-stricken girl nodded.

Andrew shook his head, hoping she was mistaken. "What happened?"

The girl gave no answer and just stared in to space.

Andrew gave her a little shove. "Tell me!"

She snapped back to reality again. "I...I don't know. She fell into the fat fryer. Got her arm all burned."

Andrew examined her expression closely. She was staring into space again as if she were incapable of eye contact.

"Bullshit!" he said to her.

The girl flinched then looked at him, but still she said nothing. More tears began to expel themselves down her cheeks.

"Frankie did this, didn't he?"

The girl shrugged off his grasp and rushed inside the chip shop, locking the door behind her. Andrew shook his head and felt tears of his own well up in his eyes.

So much for answers, he thought.

The ambulance revved its engine and started to pull away. Andrew tried to get a look in through the back windows, to see if Charlie was okay, but the glass was frosted and gave no opportunity to do so. So he stood there in shock for several minutes, praying to god that the poor girl on her way to the hospital was not hurt because of him.

Because of Frankie.

As the shock diluted into his bloodstream and faded away completely, it was replaced by a fury so alive with hatred that it seemed electrical in nature, sparking through his system and making his flesh tingle. He started for home again, wondering how he would ever explain to his family that, for the second time this week, chips were cancelled.

***

"What do you mean you're going to the hospital?" Pen asked him incredulously.

"I need to go check on someone. The girl from the chip shop told me where Frankie lives and I think he's hurt her because of it."

Pen almost spat the red wine she was drinking and had to swallow it carefully to avoid choking. "He's put the girl in hospital? Jesus Christ!"

"And it might be my fault, which is why I need to go."

Pen collapsed onto the sofa. "Crazy... This whole thing is just crazy."

Andrew sat down beside his wife and put an arm around her. "I know, but perhaps this girl will press charges and Frankie will go away again. Lord knows he deserves it."

"You want me to come with you?"

Andrew shook his head. "No, it wouldn't be fair to Charlie. She probably won't want to see me, let alone my family. You stay here and look after Bex. I think she's more upset about this situation than she lets on."

"Okay," said Pen. "Give this Charlie my best, okay?"

Andrew kissed his wife goodbye and left the house. The hospital was five or six miles away so he would need to take his car to get there. Hopefully, now that it was dark, the graffiti written all over it would not be visible. He pulled out his car keys and pressed the alarm fob. The lights flashed twice.

To the pedo-mobile, thought Andrew wryly as he looked at the once-beautiful machine. He pulled open the door and hopped inside behind the wheel, plonking his butt down onto the leather driver's seat. The ignition started as soon as he turned the key and the car was already moving when he began to fumble for his seatbelt. His eye was off the road for only a few seconds, but it was long enough to miss sight of the person standing in the road.

At only 20mph, the car was moving fast enough to launch the person up onto the bonnet and then tumbling back down to the road.

Andrew stamped on the brakes.

The tyres squealed.

The car stopped.

He stared out at the body on the road and could not believe it. His world got worse with every passing second. He pressed the release on his seat belt and shoved open the door, stepping shakily into the frosty, cold air.

He had run down a young boy, unconscious and bleeding in the road. Glass covered the asphalt with shards of glass that now sparkled in the car's headlamps like alligator teeth. Andrew rushed over to the boy and dropped down to his knees, ignoring the stabbing pains caused by the unforgiving tarmac.

"Are you okay?"

Stupid question.

"Everything is going to be okay. I'm going take you to the hospital."

I was on my way there anyway, Andrew thought grimly. To see another young kid that got hurt because of me. I'm going to hell.

Andrew sprung up off his knees and went and opened the rear passenger door of the car. Then he went back over to the injured boy, kneeled beside him, and threaded his arms underneath his shoulders to hoist him up. The weight was substantial, but thankfully the boy was pretty lean. Andrew was just about able to carry him over to the back seat of the car without running out of steam. He placed the boy down gently and bent his legs at the knee so that the door had room to close. Before Andrew had chance to close it, the boy opened his eyes and started to moan.

"Hey there," said Andrew softly. "My name is Andrew. You've been in a little accident, but everything is going to be okay. I'm taking you to the hospital right now. Can you tell me your name?"

The boy carried on moaning for a few moments more but eventually managed to answer Andrew's question. He said his name was Davie.

-8-

Andrew reached the hospital in less than ten minutes, screeching to a halt outside the entrance to the A & E department. There was no one around and he had to cry out for someone to come and help him. It wasn't long before a male nurse and a couple of orderlies appeared outside, hurrying to see what the emergency was.

The orderlies quickly retrieved a gurney and, together with the male nurse, managed to hoist Davie out of the car and onto the wheeled bed. Without hesitation they then disappeared inside the hospital with Davie, leaving Andrew alone with the male nurse.

"Do you know the boy?" the nurse asked him.

Andrew shook his head. "Said his name was Davie, but I've never met him before."

The nurse put a hand on Andrew's back and ushered him inside. "We'll take good care of him, sir. For now we'll need you to answer a few questions so that we can assess the extent of his injuries. You may have to make a report to the police as well. I assume it was you that hit him?"

It mortified Andrew to hear it out loud, but he had no choice except to nod – yes, he had hit the boy. Had run him right over because he hadn't been paying attention.

I ran down somebody's son.

The nurse led Andrew over to a grouping of cheap plastic chairs that were bolted to the floor in uniform rows. "Take a seat, sir. We'll keep you updated on his condition. Is there someone you'd like us to call?"

Andrew thought about Pen and Bex, but then found someone else popping into his head. "I need to see someone else that is already here. A girl named Charlie. She got burned today by a deep fat fryer."

The nurse raised an eyebrow. "I think I recall someone coming in with those injuries. What relation are you?"

Andrew looked down at the floor, examining the various old stains that adorned the beige tiles. "I'm...a friend."

"Okay, I'll see what I can find out for you."

Andrew thanked the man and leaned back in the chair. The bruising on his ribs throbbed as his chest compressed against the hard, uncomfortable backrest. The small waiting room was empty of people and the other chairs contained nothing other than discarded magazines and folded newspapers. Apparently, weekday evenings were not peak time for injures.

So the only two people admitted are both probably here because of me. Way to do my bit for national health.

Five minutes later, a young lady in a white tunic came and sat beside Andrew. She asked him a series of questions about the incident involving the boy and wrote down his replies on a printed form. Once she reached the end of the questionnaire, she smiled at Andrew and disappeared back into the staff only area of the hospital. Waiting for further news was a torment that he could hardly bear. For all he knew, right now, the young boy he'd hit could have permanent injuries.

The oversized clock on the waiting room wall moved along almost one full hour before someone else came to speak to him. It was the same male nurse who had met him in the car park. He sat next to Andrew. "How are you doing?"

"Not bad, considering. Any news?"

The nurse smiled and nodded. "The boy you ran into is going to be fine. He has some mild bruising on his ribs and a concussion from where his head hit the windscreen, or perhaps the road. Either way, he'll be fine after an extended rest. He was awake for a while, but he's sleeping at the moment."

Andrew let all of the air out of his lungs in a great big hiss. "Thank god. Did you let his family know?"

"No," said the nurse. "He wouldn't give us anyone to contact. He just told us to let him know when it was alright for him to leave."

"That's strange. Well, when he wakes up let him know I'm happy to drive him home."

"I'll tell him. Now about this girl you said you wanted to check on. I located her in the burns ward. She's going to be okay, but the damage to her arm is...severe."

"Permanent?" Andrew didn't really want to hear the answer.

The nurse nodded grimly. "She has second-degree burns from above her elbow all the way down her arm. She's in a great deal of pain so she's been put on morphine."

Andrew found himself unable to breathe, his bodily functions temporarily halted by the horror he was feeling.

"She's asked to see you," the nurse told him.

Andrew looked at the man. "Really?"

The nurse nodded and stood up. "I'll take you there now. She'll probably be asleep once the treatment takes hold."

Andrew stood up and followed the nurse. They passed through the waiting room for regular admittance, which was a great deal busier than the empty emergency room he had been sat in, and then continued on onto the treatment wards. They took an elevator up to the second floor and passed by the mournfully silent Oncology Department. Then they reached the Burns Unit.

The nurse pushed open one of the swinging double doors and stood aside for Andrew to enter. The first thing he noticed as he walked into the room was the suffocating odour of antiseptic creams and alcohol. The ward was cramped, divided into cubicles on both sides.

"She's in bed number three," said the nurse, pointing up ahead.

Andrew thanked the man and headed for Charlie's cubicle – a set of canvass walls and a blue nylon curtain for the door. Andrew pulled aside the curtain and stepped inside. Charlie was staring right at him when he entered.

"Hi, Charlie," he said, looking left and right for a chair to sit on. Before he found one, his eyes fixated on the thick white bandages that covered her entire left arm. He quickly broke his stare and perched himself down on a nearby chair. It was a lot comfier than the ones they had in the waiting room. "How are you doing?"

She shook her head at him wearily, obviously tired and a little out of it from the morphine that was entering through the drip on her uninjured arm. "I've been better."

"I'm really sorry you got hurt," said Andrew. "Are your parents coming?"

Charlie's voice was croaky when she spoke. "Someone's contacting them now. How come you got here so fast?"

"I ran someone over. I was already heading here to see how you were, but I guess that made me drive a little faster. I knew you'd been hurt because I was coming to the chip shop just after it happened."

Charlie let out a little laugh. It was a sleepy sound. "You hit someone?"

Andrew laughed a little too. "Yeah, if you can believe it? He's going to be fine. Which just leaves the question: what exactly happened to you?"

Charlie turned her head and looked away from him. Her eyes eventually focused on her bandaged arm. The sight seemed to upset her a great deal. "What you think?"

Andrew leaned forward on his chair. "Frankie?"

"He knew I spoke to you."

Guilt took root in Andrew's gut and started eating away at him from within, gnawing with its vicious little teeth. "I'm so sorry. I went and had it out with him this afternoon. Your friend was with him and I mentioned your name. I didn't mean for any of this to happen, you have to believe me. I was just trying to protect my..." Andrew's voice trailed off. This girl in front of him would be scarred for life. There were no excuses she needed to hear from him. None would be good enough.

"I don't want you to ever bother me again," said Charlie in a voice that was forceful despite her dreary, drug-addled tone. "This happened because of you."

"This happened because of Frankie. I know I dragged you into this, but it's him that needs to pay. We need to tell the police."

Charlie shook her head. "Frankie is a psychopath."

"I know. That's why I need you to have him arrested. I need to make sure he's stopped before...before..."

"Before he does the same to your family?"

Andrew felt sick at the thought. Earlier on, he'd been convinced that Frankie's bark was bigger than his bite but, after the callous attack on this innocent young girl, he wasn't so sure anymore.

"I'd get your family and just move," said Charlie, suddenly sounding very sleepy. "I'm not...getting...involved."

Andrew sat for a few moments, trying to formulate a counter-argument in his head but came up blank every time. Before he even came close to having something useful to say, Charlie had fallen unconscious in the grasp of morphine-soaked oblivion.

Andrew stood up. "I'm sorry," he whispered as he left the cubicle.

Outside, the male nurse who had been waiting for him asked, "Everything okay?"

Andrew shook his head. "Not at all. Can you take me to the boy I ran over please? Seems I have a lot of apologising to do this evening."

***

Andrew had to sit outside the recuperation ward for over an hour while Davie slept. He had sent a text to Pen during this time, letting her know that the girl was okay and that he would be home soon. He didn't tell her that he'd run over a young boy on the way to the hospital. That was a conversation for later.

A plump woman came out of the ward and smiled at Andrew on her way to the nurse's station nearby. As she passed she told him that, "The boy is awake now. You can go in."

Andrew nodded his thanks and stood up. His knees clicked as they straightened out and he suddenly felt sixty years old as he headed for the ward. Inside, there were a dozen separate beds, half of them empty. At the far end was the boy he'd hit, head wrapped in a bright-white bandage. Andrew walked over and stood at the end of the bed.

"How you doing?" asked Andrew. "You feeling okay?"

The boy's eyes went very wide for a split-second, almost as if he recognised Andrew, but that seemed unlikely. "Y-yeah, thanks. Was it you that ran me over?"

Andrew nodded.

"Did you do it on purpose?"

"What?" Andrew's mouth fell open. "Of course not. I never meant it at all. I'm really sorry this happened."

The boy was silent for a moment as if trying to work something out in his head. "Okay. So you never wanted to hurt me?"

"Of course not. I've never even met you before. I'm sorry, okay?"

The boy nodded. "Thanks. I was probably to blame anyway. I was running across the road without looking."

Andrew smiled and shrugged his shoulders. "Well, whoever's to blame it was just an accident. You're going to be okay and that's the main thing. I'm happy to give you a ride home when you're ready, pal?"

"No, no, that's okay. I'll make it home on my own."

"Don't be silly," said Andrew. "I hit you five miles from here. I'm not letting you make your own way home with a concussion."

"But-"

"No arguments. I'll go talk to the nurses now and see if we can break you out of here. Then we can go get a McDonalds on the way home or something."

The boy smiled. "They said I'm not allowed to eat for twenty-four hours."

Andrew winked at the boy. "Who's going to know?"

"Okay," said Davie. "Thanks."

"Sure thing. Where am I driving you to anyway?"

The boy seemed to hesitate before he answered. "T-Tanner's Avenue."

Andrew raised an eyebrow. "Tanner's Avenue? Great...I know the place. I'll be waiting outside for you, okay?"

Andrew left Davie alone and exited the ward, wondering whether or not coincidences really existed.

-9-

Davie was almost certain that the man waiting for him outside the ward was the very same guy who had been on his doorstep earlier arguing with Frankie. While not one hundred per cent positive, Davie recognised that the man had the same neat, brown hair and spindly posture.

He pulled on his jeans behind the plastic wraparound curtain of his cubicle, and every time he peeked through the gap in the sheet, he could see the man peering in at him through the long windows of the ward.

Waiting to batter me to death and finish what he started when he ran me down with his car.

Davie didn't believe that, though. The man – Andrew, was it? – didn't seem to mean any harm. In fact, it didn't seem like the man even knew who Davie was – or who his brother happened to be. Davie thought about the word *coincidence* and decided that it was the correct one for this situation. Still, what would happen when the man dropped him off at the same house he'd been at earlier?

There was no chance of him letting Davie make his own way home – he felt too responsible – so the best plan would be to have him stop and drop him off at the end of Tanner's Avenue. Davie could pretend to walk to another house then go home when the coast was clear.

He pushed his feet into his worn trainers and suddenly felt dizzy. He fell back onto the bed and closed his eyes until the feeling passed. The bump on his head throbbed rhythmically and each time it did he felt a little more nauseated. The thought of telling his mother or Frankie that he'd been in an accident made him feel even more ill.

Frankie would go mad, especially if he found out who was responsible.

After a few moments of remaining still, the sickness went away, so Davie pulled aside the privacy curtain and stepped away from the bed. The man was still waiting outside and gave a little wave through the window. There was a young woman in a nurse's uniform standing beside him.

Davie pushed through the ward's double doors and the nurse held something out to him – a small plastic container. "Take these pills every morning," she said, "and at lunchtime. They should help with the headaches. You need absolute rest so get yourself in bed, sweetheart, and don't leave for anything, you hear? You have someone to look after you?"

Davie lied. "Yeah, my mum."

"Let's get you home, then," said the man, wrapping an arm around Davie's shoulders and ushering him away. It made Davie uncomfortable to be touched by an adult, but he did not resist.

"You really don't have to take me, Mr..."

"I do," he said firmly, "and you can call me Andrew. You're my responsibility until I get you home. Still fancy that McDonalds?"

Davie thought about the recurring sickness that constantly rose in his tummy and shook his head. "Thanks all the same, but I think it will just make me feel worse. I just want to go home to bed."

"No probs. I'm parked right outside so I'll have you there in ten."

The two of them set off through the bleak corridors of the hospital, the silence growing more awkward with each passing step. Davie considered making a run for it, but knew he wouldn't make it more than a few yards without having to throw up. Just strolling along like this took effort.

"This way," said Andrew, just as Davie was about to make a turn into the reception area. "I came in through the A&E not General Admissions."

Davie followed Andrew into a waiting room that was empty except for a young lad with a thick clump of glass sticking out of a bleeding head wound. He was sobbing to himself quietly as he sat there alone.

Someone's bottled him, Davie thought to himself, knowing the type of injury well from experience. The scars never completely go away.

Davie and Andrew exited the hospital and stepped into the cold breeze of the car park. There was a bright red Mercedes parked askew across several parking bays and, as Davie got closer, he could see that the vehicle was plastered in graffiti – the words Pedo Pedo Pedo written all over it. Davie glanced at Andrew uncertainly.

Andrew seemed to realise the situation and immediately became flustered, waving his hands and shaking his head defensively. "No, no, no, you don't need to worry. That's just the work of some idiot that's been terrorising the neighbourhood. His idea of a joke!"

"Ha ha," said Davie without inflection; secretly thinking that Frankie had a weird sense of humour. "You must have laughed all night?"

Andrew looked at Davie and then suddenly broke into laughter. "Yeah, I had an absolute hoot. Now, come on, get yourself inside the pedo-wagon. I want to take you home and show you my basement."

Davie joined in the laughter and pulled open the passenger door once Andrew had disengaged the automatic locks. Despite the spoiled paintwork, it was the poshest car he'd ever been in. The seats were soft, stitched from leather, and the dashboard had a sleek metallic sheen that was peppered with chrome-plated dials and switches.

"Nice motor," he commented.

"Thanks," said Andrew, sliding into the driver's seat and strapping himself in. "I only just got it, but I think it's nice too. Obviously someone felt it needed some custom paintwork."

"Will it cost a lot to repair?"

Andrew started the engine and looked forward. He shrugged. "I imagine so. Hopefully my insurance will cover it, but then they charge you more every month to make up for it."

"That sucks," said Davie, not really understanding the ins and outs of motor insurance, but assuming it was a big rip-off like everything else. "You know who did it?"

Andrew nodded but said nothing.

Davie shifted slightly in his seat as the car began moving out of the hospital car park. "You going to do anything about it? To the person that did it, I mean?"

"Don't know," said Andrew. "Don't know if there's anything I can do."

Davie frowned. "What do you mean?"

"I mean that I'm a good man. I look after my family and go to work so that I can give them a good life, but what can I do if someone decides to make my life hell? The police won't help me and I don't know how to fight worth a damn. Seems to me that it's all too easy to be a thug nowadays."

The car pulled onto a main road and picked up speed. The powerful engine purred proudly. There was no other traffic that Davie could see. The dashboard's digital clock said that it was a little after nine at night, which explained the empty roads.

"Maybe he'll leave you alone once he's had his fun?" Davie proposed.

"Sounds like you know something about it? You don't go around terrorising people do you?"

Davie shook his head without even thinking about it. You always pled innocent, no matter what. "No, I don't want to hurt anyone," he said, "but I've known people who do?"

The car sped up as it entered a slip road to a carriageway. "Really? Like who?"

Davie shrugged, wondering to himself why exactly he had even instigated this conversation in the first place. "Just kids I've hung around with," he said. "At school and that, you know?"

Andrew nodded as if he understood. "You enjoy school?"

"Hate it, but I try my best anyway. I promised my mum I would get a job and not end up like my brother.

Oh shit, why did he say that?

"You have a brother?"

Davie swallowed what felt like a huge lump in his throat. "Yeah. He...moved away, years ago now, but he was always up to no good."

"Hurting people?" said Andrew.

Davie thought about how loud Charlie had screamed when Frankie held her arm in the chip fat. It was the hottest thing Davie had ever seen, bubbling and spitting like molten agony. The young girl cried out so loudly when her hand had touched it that something must have given way inside her throat. The tone of her voice changed pitch mid-scream. Frankie had broken his own rule about never hurting a woman and the whole incident had sent Davie's world spiralling. The violence made him feel woozy, so he'd run. Run away from the chip shop as fast as he could. Then something had hit him like a ton of bricks. Next thing he knew, he was waking up in a hospital with a nurse bandaging his head.

Even now, Davie had a hard time accepting what had happened in the chip shop. The old Frankie he had grown up with would never have hurt a defenceless girl like that. The old Frankie he grew up with would not have done a lot of the things he had been doing lately.

"...kay?"

Davie looked up from his thoughts. "Huh?"

"I said, are you okay?"

"Yeah." Davie nodded. "Just feel a bit sick."

Andrew turned to him and smiled. "We're almost there now. Hold on."

Davie decided not to participate in any further conversation. The less Andrew knew about him – and his blood relatives – the better. In fact, too much had been said already.

The speeding car took a road on the left and started slowing down. It entered into a residential area that Davie did not recognise.

"I think you've gone the wrong way."

Andrew shook his head, but kept his eyes forward. "No, I haven't"

"Yeah, you have," Davie argued. "You should have kept on the main road for a little while longer, I think."

"We're making a little detour first."

Davie felt sick. "What?"

Andrew smiled at Davie for a moment then looked back at the road. "I have someone I want you to meet. Then I will take you home, alright?"

"Okay," Davie hesitated. "Who?"

Andrew took a deep breath as if he was considering something. "I want you to meet my family, Davie. They were worried when I told them I hit you. I just want them to see that you're okay. That cool, buddy?"

Davie nodded. "Yeah, okay, but I really need to get home soon."

"No problem. Be five minutes. My wife will never get off my back until she knows you're going to be okay."

Davie looked out of the window as the car parked up on the curb outside of a row of houses. He couldn't help feeling like a rat caught in a trap. There was something off about the situation and Andrew's demeanour had suddenly changed, but Davie had nowhere to run. Couldn't run.

Andrew applied the parking brake and switched off the ignition. "Okay, get out."

Davie nodded in silence. He pushed open the door on his side and stepped out into the street. The air felt icy after leaving the stifling compartment of the car. It was a good sensation, though, and woke up his senses, easing the low-level headache that had been with him since the hospital.

"Come on, inside," said Andrew, walking up a path to one of the houses. There was a light on in the living room, mingling with the pulsing flash of a television.

Davie followed obediently, wishing he was somewhere else – anywhere else – than the property of a man who most likely meant him harm.

Andrew opened the front door with a key and stepped inside. Dave stepped inside too, stopping inside the porch.

"Living room's on the left, buddy. Go on through."

Davie entered the hallway and turned to the door on the left. It felt as though turning the handle would be the beginning of something he didn't want to get into. He wanted to refuse to go in, to turn around and demand to be let out. But it was too late for that.

He was already inside.

Davie turned the handle and pushed open the door, then entered the living room. Inside, there was a mixture of smells that didn't usually go together. It smelt like vinegar and...bleach? A moment later Davie saw the source of each odour. Two women – one young and one older – crawled on their hands and knees, scrubbing at the carpet with bleach-soaked cloths. The whole room seemed to be littered with mashed up potatoes and bits of fish.

"My family," said Andrew behind him.

The women looked up and both seemed to receive a fright at Davie's presence. Both of them stood up quickly.

Andrew stepped through into the centre of the living room and stood in front of the women. "This is just one of the things Frankie has done to us for no reason, Davie. My wife and daughter have been scrubbing at these carpets all day and the smell still hasn't gone completely. You know all about the damage to my car."

Davie shook his head and wondered what to say. What words would make this situation end?

The older woman's eyes had gone wide and she looked at him, bewildered. "You know Frankie?"

Davie said nothing. He didn't want to admit to anything that could get him hurt.

"This is Frankie's brother," said Andrew, "and he's a good lad."

Davie raised an eyebrow at him. "What?"

Andrew shrugged. "Maybe I'm wrong, but I don't think you enjoy hurting people like your brother does."

Davie still chose to say nothing. His thoughts were a muddle, perhaps from the concussion – perhaps not.

"Sit down," said the woman. "I'll get us all some tea."

Davie hesitated. He still wanted out of there, but somehow felt his uneasiness going away at the thought of staying. A cup of tea sounded nice. They never had any milk at home.

The younger girl stepped towards Davie and held out her hand. She was about his age and beautiful – like a younger version of her mother but with a lightness to her features that made her seem angelic. Davie could tell just by looking at her that she was a kind person. She continued to offer out her hand and Davie finally took it, albeit reluctantly.

"My name's Rebecca," she said, leading him towards the sofa. "Take a seat and we'll talk things through. You look like you've been in the wars."

Davie sat down and nodded. "I got run over."

Rebecca sat beside him and looked shocked. "No way!"

"Yes," said Andrew, seating himself on a nearby armchair. "It was me who hit him."

The girl now seemed even more shocked.

"Was an accident, Bex," Andrew added. "Davie's going to be just fine, so don't worry."

"Thank god. This week's been horrible enough without anything else happening."

"I'm sorry," said Davie without realising the word was going to escape his lips.

"It's okay," Rebecca told him. "We just want your brother to leave us alone."

"Yes," said Andrew. "It all needs to stop, right now. We're innocent people."

The older woman reentered the room with a tray full of steaming mugs. The one she handed to Davie had a Bart Simpson design. "I added sugar. Is that okay?"

Davie nodded and thanked her, but then said, "I need to go home."

"Okay," Andrew nodded. "Just drink your tea and we'll get going. I just wanted you to meet my girls first."

"Why?"

"So that you can tell your brother that we're real people he's hurting."

"He knows that."

"Does he? Because maybe things don't seem as real if you don't know the person you're having fun with."

Davie shrugged. "I know what you're doing, but I don't think it will work. I'm sorry."

"Can you not do anything at all, Davie?" asked the mother.

Davie shook his head. "Frankie doesn't listen to anyone, least of all me. I think... I think he enjoys hurting people."

Andrew nodded. "Like Charlie."

Davie looked down at the liquid in the mug and watched it steam. "I don't know what you're talking about. I just want to go home. If you take me now, I won't tell Frankie about what happened."

Andrew raised an eyebrow at him. "Are you threatening me?"

Davie shrugged. "Guess I am. Frankie has got it in for you. If he hears that you ran me over, I don't know what he'll do."

"So why would you want to tell him if it will cause more trouble?"

Davie stood up, flinging his mug of steaming tea aside, adding to the stains on the carpet. "Because you won't let me the fuck go. I've asked you nicely. Now let me fucking leave, right now, you get me?" Davie felt woozy, but continued anyway. "I'll walk home from here and not say a thing, but if you keep me here any longer, you'll pay."

Andrew's eyes saddened as they looked at him. He stood up and nodded. "Okay, son. It's a shame because I thought better of you. Guess I had it wrong. Maybe it's the concussion talking."

Davie couldn't understand why, but tears began to beat at the back of his eyelids. Andrew had been correct when he said knowing a victim makes things more real. It upset him to see the effects of Frankie's behaviour, but it was none of his business. Frankie was family. Frankie was his brother. This man in front of him was just a stranger.

Davie yanked open the door to the hallway and stepped outside, trying to control his breathing as it threatened to get out of control. He entered the porch and waited for Andrew to come and unlock the front door. It was not Andrew, however, that came to join him. It was Rebecca.

"Hi," she said to him.

Davie gave a half-smile. "Hey," he said back. "I'm sorry about all this shit my brother's brought down on you, but it's nothing to do with me."

Rebecca smiled at him and nodded, then reached out a hand and touched his shoulder. "It's okay. I know you can't do anything about it. It was shitty of my dad to corner you like that, but he's just trying to protect us, you know?"

Davie didn't want to get into it anymore. He just wanted to leave. He found himself giving an answer, though. "I understand why he did it and I'm not going to tell anyone. Just let me out, okay?"

Rebecca obliged. She produced a key from her pocket and shimmied past him.

Her body felt warm against his as she brushed past and Davie felt dizzy again. She unlocked the door for him and stood aside.

"Thanks," he told her, taking one last look at her – sad that they would not speak again after this. Just as he stepped out onto the pathway, she put a hand out and stopped him. "It's okay, you know?"

"What's okay?"

"Being afraid of Frankie. I am too. I guess lots of people are."

Davie puffed up his shoulders. "I'm not afraid of anybody. Especially not my own brother."

Rebecca nodded and smiled at him, almost like she pitied him now. "If you're not afraid, then why won't you help us?"

Davie was thinking of an answer when he heard someone shout from behind him. It was his brother's voice. Frankie was there.

"Davie? The fuck are you doing here? Why the hell are you coming out of that fucker's house?"

-10-

Andrew heard Bex scream and immediately panicked. His first thought was that he'd completely misjudged Davie, and that the boy had done something to hurt her. He pushed past Pen and raced into the hallway. Bex was still crying when he got there but she didn't seem to be hurt. In fact she was alone.

"Bex, what the hell is going on?"

She spun around. "It's Frankie. He's outside."

Andrew stepped up to the front door and looked out into the night. Davie was halfway down the path. Frankie was with him and the two were arguing – both voices heated and angry, but the sound of Davie's voice seemed to be more pleading than it was aggressive.

"What the fuck happened to you, bro?" Frankie demanded, pointing to the bandage on Davie's head. "Did that fuckin' mug give you a kicking? He's a dead man."

"No," said Davie. "I got hit by a car. The guy who lives here was just helping me. He took me to the hospital and drove me back."

Frankie looked towards the house and spotted Andrew standing there. "Oh, did he? Is that what you do, old man? Give lifts to young boys?"

Andrew moved Bex back and told her to go and join her mother in the living room. Then he looked back at Frankie. "He was injured. Would you have preferred I just left him there?"

Frankie didn't say anything and Andrew hoped that he was getting through to him at last. When he eventually did speak, it was in a calmer tone than usual. "No, course not, but how the hell did you happen to be there anyway?"

"Right time, right place," said Davie.

But Andrew owned up. He couldn't rely on Davie to keep his secret. "Because it was me who hit him, Frankie. It was an accident and that's why I made sure he got to the hospital. I'm very sorry about it all, but your brother is a sweet boy and I'm glad to have met him. Maybe we should all go inside and talk."

Frankie's face dropped. "You mowed down my little brother? You're a dead man." He marched up the path, shoving aside his brother's attempts to stop him. "A motherfuckin' dead man."

Andrew stood rooted in the doorway, unsure how to proceed. When Frankie pulled out a flick knife and released the blade, the decision was obvious. He slammed shut the front door and locked it as quickly as he could. Then he called the police.

***

Frankie had stood outside the house for almost ten minutes, screaming threats and vowing that Andrew would pay for what he'd done. Bex and Pen were both in tears by the time he finally went away. Five minutes later, the police arrived and were now sitting in the living room again. It was the same two officers, Dalton and Wardsley.

"He actually threatened your life," asked Wardsley.

Andrew nodded. "Several times. My entire family heard him. Then he pulled a knife on me."

"Okay. I think we have good reason to go and ask this Frankie a few questions now."

"Questions," said Andrew, leaning forward in his armchair. "I want you to do more than that. He's a danger to society."

Wardsley nodded. "I understand you want something done, sir. Believe me, we'll be arresting him and holding him overnight. We'll do what we can to get him in front of a judge, but..."

Andrew nodded. "But he'll be back on the street in twenty-four hours, regardless."

Dalton took over for her partner. "Exactly. I'm afraid that's the system. The burden of proof is on the victim, not the offender. He'll be free until convicted."

Andrew flopped back in his chair. All the times he had dismissed conservative claims that there was too little justice in the British prosecution system and it turns out they were right. There was no justice. Andrew's family were being terrorised and the system would do nothing to immediately protect them. Andrew didn't blame the two police officers in his living room. They'd let down their impersonal barriers since the last time they'd visited and seemed genuinely sympathetic now. Andrew imagined they were just as frustrated by their lack of power as he himself was. Their jobs were to give a court ammunition, but courts were slow and indifferent.

"Look," said Andrew. "What the hell should I do?"

"Do you have anyone you can stay with?" Dalton asked.

Andrew shrugged. "I guess. Pen's parents could have us for a while, but how does that help in the long run?"

"It will just be until we bring Frankie in front of a judge."

"But you don't think I have much of a case. Not enough evidence."

PC Dalton bit at her lip before sighing. "All you have is threats. It's not enough. The Forensics didn't find much either, I'm afraid."

"So, what then?"

The two officers thought for a moment. Eventually it was Dalton who said something. "Look," she said. "I'll make a phone call to the Super and see what we can do. I would strongly suggest leaving in the morning and going somewhere else for a while. In the meantime we'll get this piece of scum off the streets and make it clear to him that we're watching his every move."

"And will you be?" asked Andrew.

Dalton shrugged. "I'll request a plain-clothes to be stationed in the area. Hopefully if we supervise Frankie's movements long enough, we'll catch him doing something illegal."

Andrew felt himself relax, tension flooding out of his bones in great heaps. Someone being nearby watching over his family was exactly what he wanted. If Frankie tried anything else, there would be a witness – a police witness.

"Thank you," said Andrew, standing up and offering out his hand. "That's exactly what I wanted to hear. It's such a relief."

The police officers stood up and Wardsley shook his hand. "Don't get too excited just yet. We'll fight a good case for you, but it's not our decision at the end of the day."

Andrew nodded. "Okay, but you'll let me know?"

"Of course, but you should stay somewhere else in the meantime, until we figure things out. Even if we do get a man put on Frankie, it will still take a couple of days."

"Well, you have my thanks just for doing anything at all. I was beginning to think that I'd never get help."

Wardsley seemed a little irritated by his comment, but Andrew felt it was fair and didn't apologise for it.

"We do our best Mr Goodman, but we can only do as the law allows. We'll let ourselves out."

Andrew nodded and stood aside. He was too relieved to feel guilty for offending the officers. In his opinion, it wasn't asking too much for a little help from the police service – but again he reminded himself that it was likely not their fault.

He turned back into the living room and found Pen and Bex standing there. Obviously they'd been eavesdropping from the kitchen.

Pen put her arms around him and squeezed tight. "That's a relief, ay?"

Andrew hugged her right back and kissed the top of her forehead. "Yeah, maybe we can go back to normal now. I'll call work and get a few days off. They won't like it but tough-titties. We'll go stay with your parents till the end of next week. Then we'll come home and play things by ear."

"A whole week with Nan and Granddad," said Bex with a frown. "Seriously?"

Andrew stuck out his tongue playfully. "You'll live. They don't see enough of you anyway. We can sit around in our PJs all day watching horror movies if you want."

"You don't like horror movies. They scare you."

Andrew nodded. "After this week, I think real life is scarier."

"No one is lazing around in their PJs," said Pen. "I don't want my parents thinking we're a bunch of slobs. We can go on some daytrips. Leicester zoo is a nice afternoon out. They have a silverback gorilla there called Nero."

"Sounds like a plan," said Andrew. "Guess we should go pack."

Pen laughed and walked toward the kitchen. "At least let me go call them first. They might not have us."

"Here's hoping," said Bex.

Andrew slapped his daughter on the bum. "Behave."

Bex held up her hands in two fists. "You don't got what it takes to beat me, old man. You're nothing but a lousy bum."

Andrew grinned. "You reckon?"

Bex nodded and giggled.

"We'll see about that." Andrew lunged for his daughter, making her shriek and run upstairs in a fit of giggles. A minute later her dreadful pop music came on her stereo and thudded through the living room ceiling. Looked like things were back to normal already.

There were no guarantees that his encounters with Frankie were truly over, but at least now there would be consequences if he were to try anything else. At least for the next week-and-a-half they would be away from the worry. Hopefully his bosses would understand. The project he was working on could wait a little while longer.

Best I call them now, Andrew thought, heading for the phone in the kitchen. Pen intercepted him on her way out and put her hand up to stop him.

"I'm just going to call the firm," he told her, wondering why she had blocked his path.

She shook her head. "The phone isn't working."

Andrew wrinkled his brow. "Really? Let me have a look."

The two of them went into the kitchen and Andrew headed over to the fridge. On the wall beside it was the cordless phone in its cradle. Andrew plucked the handset free and held it to his ear.

Nothing.

There was no dial tone at all. He keyed in some numbers to see if they made any noise on the line. They did not.

Andrew placed the handset back down and tried to figure it out. First he checked that the phone line was connected into the cradle and found that it was. Next he decided to verify that the phone line was connected at the wall output. He followed the cream-coloured wire downwards towards the floor and then began tracing it along the skirting board. The wire disappeared behind the fridge, but he found it coming out the other side. It was on the other side of the fridge that Andrew discovered the reason why the phone was no longer working.

"The line's been cut."

Pen looked at him blankly, then down at the skirting board. "What? How?"

Andrew stared at the frayed wire and could think of only one reason. "We need to get out of here now. Frankie's been inside the house again."

"What? You think he did this?"

"Look at the wire, Pen. It didn't cut itself!"

Pen went white; a ghostly pallor consuming her usually flushed features. "Where's your mobile? Call the officers, they only just left."

Andrew nodded and rushed back into the living room. His phone was on the coffee table. He'd put it there when the officers had been questioning him. When he went for it, he found that it was gone. Not only was his phone missing, but also the coffee table it had been sitting on was now upended.

Pen came up behind him, a little too close, and made him flinch. He turned to her and put his hands on each of her shoulders. "You, me, and Rebecca are getting in the car right now. He's in the house."

Pen nodded and followed him without argument as he rushed across the living room. "Rebecca," he shouted in the hallway. "Get down here now."

There was no reply.

Panic blasted through Andrew's veins.

There was a knock at the front door.

Andrew stared at his wife, who stared back at him like a rabbit caught in the headlights of a speeding truck. She spoke. "It could be the police. They only just left."

Andrew considered the possibility and decided it was viable.

The door knocked again.

Andrew looked back up the stairs. "Bex, are you up there?"

Still no answer.

Andrew made a decision and entered the porch, opened the front door.

It was not the police officers that were standing there.

Two black youths stood in front of Andrew, identical in appearance. The twins from Frankie's gang. A voice came from behind him and he spun around. Frankie stood at the top of the stairs, holding Bex around the throat from behind. She was shaking and sobbing.

"Call the cops on me? Big mistake." Frankie pushed Bex forward. Her bare feet found nothing but air and she fell, hitting the steps and tumbling awkwardly to the bottom. There was the sickening sound of something snapping.

Before Andrew had chance to react, something struck the back of his head and his world went dark.

-11-

Davie followed Dom and Jordan into the house with Michelle trailing behind them. Frankie was already inside, standing over the unconscious bodies of both Andrew and his daughter. The mother was screaming out hysterically for help.

"Sort that bitch out, will ya?"

Davie realised that Frankie was talking to him, but found himself unable to do anything other than just stand there with his mouth agape.

Frankie pushed him. "Sort the bitch out now, before she brings attention."

"W-what you want me to do?"

Frankie shook his head impatiently. "What you think I want you to do, you mug? Take her into the living room and shut her goddamn mouth."

Davie nodded and took the woman away, holding her gently by the arm. She didn't struggle, but neither did she cease her screaming. They entered the living room and he eased her down onto the couch.

"You gotta be quiet," he told her in what he hoped was a soothing voice. "Frankie will kick off if you don't."

The woman carried on shouting out for help, but slowly her words were becoming a continuous, garbled slur. Gradually her volume lowered.

Davie patted her on the back. "That's it. Just try to calm down. Would you like a cup of tea?"

Frankie entered the room. "You kidding me? Why don't you bake her a cake as well."

Davie stood up and faced his brother. "I'm just trying to calm her down. That's what you wanted, isn't it?"

"Just keep an eye on her."

Davie nodded and sat back down beside the woman. Frankie moved behind an armchair in the room and shoved it forward along the carpet. Then he went and drew the curtains shut and turned down the lights with the dimmer switch.

"There," said Frankie. "The mood is set. Bring 'em in, lads."

Dom and Jordan entered the room, dragging Andrew and Bex along the floor. Andrew had woken slightly since Dom had struck him in the back of the head, but was still pretty much out of it, eyes swirling around in their sockets and unable to focus.

"Get him up onto the armchair," said Frankie. "Come on, come on."

Dom and Jordan hoisted Andrew up onto the armchair and propped up his head, which kept sagging against his chest.

"Where's the tape?" asked Frankie. His twitch was acting up.

Dom and Jordan both shrugged in unison, the fact that they were twins making it look like some weird double-act. "Think Shell has it," said Jordan.

Frankie shook his head and cursed beneath his breath. "Michelle! Get your skinny ass in here."

It was a couple of minutes before she appeared, but when she did Davie saw that she did indeed have the thick roll of silver duct tape in her hand.

Frankie snatched it from her. "What the hell were you doing?"

Michelle shrugged her bony shoulders. "Just having a look around. There's some nice stuff in the girl's room. Look." She held up her right hand, which now sported a shiny gem on the ring finger. "Bet it belonged to her Nan or something. Sad bitch keeps a diary too; had a quick read and it was hilarious. Says she's still afraid of the dark."

"Very nice," said Frankie in a way that made it clear he didn't give a shit. He turned to Andrew and pointed. "Dom, get this fucker strapped up. I want him to be nice and comfortable when we get the party started. He'll have the best seat in the house."

Davie sat silently on the sofa, wondering what his brother meant. He had a feeling that whatever he thought would not be as bad as whatever Frankie actually had in mind. In a competition for sickest imagination, Davie's big brother won every time.

Dom finished taping up Andrew just as he started to stir from unconsciousness. A thin stream of drool fell from his mouth and pooled on the tape that secured his midsection to the chair.

"Wakey wakey, rise and shine," said Frankie, laughing at himself afterwards. "I was wondering if Dom had ended you with the smack he gave you. Glad he didn't, as this will be a whole lot more fun with you alive."

Andrew managed to lift his head and look Frankie in the eyes. "W-what... are you going to do?"

Frankie leaned forward so that his eye line matched Andrew's own. "Tell the truth, I haven't decided yet. Don't you worry, though. It's going to be a good crack."

Andrew's wife whimpered and Davie patted her on the back again to quiet her down.

"Why are you doing this to us, you...you monster?" Andrew managed to ask.

"Not us," said Frankie. "I'm doing this to you. The ladies are just unlucky to be involved with you. Collateral damage, is that what they say?"

"So why...are you doing this to me?"

Frankie shrugged. "I don't like your face."

Andrew shook his head and another sliver of drool escaped his mouth. "There must be a reason."

Frankie swung his arm and struck Andrew in his ribs. His wife cried out, while he cried inwards, sucking in a breath and finding himself unable to let it out again. Frankie grabbed a bunch of his hair and lifted his head to face him. "Shut it."

"Leave him alone," Andrew's wife screamed before Davie had chance to stop her.

Frankie glared. "Or else what, bitch?"

"My name is not bitch. It's Penelope, and you're nothing but a pathetic bully."

Frankie looked around the room, mock offended. Everyone laughed hysterically. "Check this one out. Ten seconds ago she was behaving quite nicely and being a good girl. Now she's grown a big fat set of balls. You want to take me on, sweetheart?"

"Just be quiet," Davie whispered in the mother's ear.

"That's it," said Frankie. "Listen to my baby brother. He'll keep you safe."

Michelle sidled up to Frankie and draped herself on him. Davie could tell that she'd snorted a line of coke recently. Her eyes were bloodshot and wide as dinner plates, while her lips constantly puckered as though she had a mouth full of ash. "What's the plan then, honey?" she asked. "We gunna to party or what?"

Frankie kissed her hard on the mouth and then pushed her down onto the sofa beside Penelope. "Yeah, baby. It's going to get real, but we have all night, so just settle in and get some gear on the go."

"That's what I'm talking about," said Dom, hopping up and down. Jordan was in agreement and slapped his twin on the back.

"Before we do that, though," said Frankie. "Let's get the women-folk sorted. Last thing we need is them getting away." He turned to Davie. "Get the old bird taped up, little bro."

Davie stared at his brother to make sure he was serious. "She won't do anything, Frankie. I'll watch her."

Frankie grabbed the tape off Dom and threw it at Davie. "I'm getting real sick of your arguing, man. Just do what I'm telling you and tape the old bag up."

Davie stared at his brother a while longer, but realised he was pushing Frankie's patience, so he turned away and pulled off a strip of tape. "I'm sorry," he told Penelope, and then began to tape her up.

She didn't resist, but the whole time he wrapped the tape around her she looked at him with utter hatred. It made Davie feel wretched inside. As soon as he was done, he stood up and moved over to his brother who was peeking out of a gap in the curtains.

"What you want, little bro?" Frankie asked as Davie approached. He didn't turn away from the window.

"How you know it was me?"

"Cus it seems like lately every time I turn around you're on my back."

"Just looking out for you."

Frankie let the curtain go and turned around. "I know you are. You're my blood, bro, and that means more than anything. But you keep riding me and we gunna have a problem. You get me?"

Davie nodded. He tried to swallow but found himself unable.

"You don't need to worry about me," Frankie continued. "I got my shit tight – wrapped up solid."

Davie turned and looked at Andrew in the armchair. "They'll go to the cops as soon as you let them go. You'll end up back inside."

Frankie smirked. "You see? That's where you underestimate me, little bro. Who said I'm going to let them go?"

Frankie moved away from the window, leaving Davie to think about what his brother intended. He looked around the living room at Andrew and his family: Bex unconscious and her mother taped up and frightened. Then he looked at Michelle, the twins, and his brother. He knew right then that he was different to them all – the odd one out. Unlike them, he was not enjoying any of this. Not enjoying it at all.

-12-

Andrew looked down at his daughter and fought the urge to cry. He would not give these thugs the satisfaction. He knew now that he had indeed heard something snap as his precious child had been callously pushed down the stairs. Her left wrist was purple from the subdural bleeding almost certainly caused by a broken bone. Agony would consume her when she awoke and Andrew hoped with all his heart that she slept till this was all over.

But when would that be, and what will have happened in the meantime?

Andrew watched Frankie, who was kneeling beside the coffee table and emptying a small plastic bag onto the glass surface. A small pile of fine white powder began building up. Frankie's girlfriend – Michelle – was kneeling beside him with a small makeup mirror and using it to sweep the substance into several parallel lines. The twins stood watching nearby like baying dogs, almost drooling at the sight of the powder in front of them.

Then there was Davie, Frankie's younger brother. Andrew watched the boy sitting beside Pen and couldn't work him out. He was as complicit in this as the rest of them, but something about the expression on his face expressed that he was not enjoying himself.

While everyone was busy doing other things, Andrew took the opportunity to test his bonds. He wriggled side to side, trying to loosen the adhesion of the duct tape that bound him to the chair. At first, the tape started to give a little, but then the plastic bunched up and became unbreakable. There was no chance of getting free.

Which meant he was fucked.

Frankie and his entourage began snorting the lines of white powder off the coffee table, noses twitching frantically as the substance entered their bodies. Frankie's regular twitch had now gone into overdrive.

"That's good shit," said one of the twins, either Dom or Jordan. "Buzzin'."

"Innit," said Michelle. "Fuckin' heaven."

"Not too much," Frankie told them. "We can't zone out when there's shit to be taken care of."

Michelle cackled maliciously then sauntered over towards Andrew. She patted him on the cheek hard enough that it was almost a slap. "You ready to party, old man? You want some of this?" She rubbed her fingers against Andrew's lips and forced past to his gums. He tasted the powder on her fingernails and then suddenly his entire mouth went numb. He spat.

Michelle removed her hand from his mouth and stared him dead in the eye, but Andrew said nothing. There was no telling how far these messed-up teenagers were prepared to go, so best not to provoke them. Andrew looked across at Pen. She had the same anxious expression on her face that he no doubt wore on his, but there was something else in her expression that spoke of a steely determination to not give in to these thugs.

Our home, thought Andrew. The place we're supposed to feel safe. I won't let a bunch of uncontrollable kids take that away from us.

Frankie switched the television on and turned up the volume, gave Andrew a catlike grin. "Don't want people hearing the screams, do we?"

Andrew swallowed a lump in his throat. Things were about to begin, he could feel it; like sitting on a rollercoaster about to take that first horrifying plunge.

Michelle clapped her hands together. "Sweet! Friends has just started. That shit is so funny."

Frankie pulled Michelle's arm so that she spun to face him. "We're not here to watch Ross bloody shag that skank, Rachel."

Michelle's smile slunk away and she nodded like a chastised child.

Frankie really had a hold on these kids. What a difference a few years of age made. They almost seemed to look up to him like a father.

"You guys keep an eye on things," Frankie said. "I'm going to check out the kitchen."

"What for?" Davie asked him, an apprehensive tone to his voice.

Frankie ruffled his brother's hair. "Just going to look for some munchies."

He disappeared into the kitchen and somehow the room felt empty without him, like an atmosphere of oppression and danger had left the room. Andrew took the opportunity to speak without his presence. "Davie, you have to stop this? We've done nothing to you."

Davie shook his head and didn't reply – his expression was tormented.

"Davie!" Andrew repeated.

A slap stung his cheek, rattling his entire face. It was one of the twins who hit him. "Shut the fuck up, bitch, or I'll mess you up bad."

"Nice one, Dom," said the other twin. Andrew noticed a slight difference between them now. The other twin, Jordan, had a wispy goatee growing on his chin, whilst Dom was clean-shaven. Dom also wore a sovereign ring, which had been attached to the hand that had slapped Andrew. He could feel a throbbing bruise forming already.

"What do you get out of this?" Andrew directed the question to all of them.

"Shits-n-giggles," Dom replied. "Now shut it, or else."

"Or else what? You're going to do what you want to do anyway."

"Yeah, but we can make it hurt a lot worse," said Frankie re-entering the room. "So don't get on our tits." He was clasping a pair of scissors that he must've gotten from one of the kitchen drawers. The blades were long and glinted under the soft light of the living room. "Before the party starts we need to get everyone looking presentable." He pointed the scissors at Pen. "And I think this old bag is in serious need of a haircut."

The teenagers cheered, except for Davie who seemed like he was trying to force a smile but couldn't quite manage it.

"Leave my wife alone," Andrew shouted.

Frankie ignored the outburst and grabbed ahold of Pen's hair. She squealed, making a tormented sound that Andrew had not heard from her before and would be happy to never hear again. He screamed again at Frankie, ordering him to get out of his home, but the demands fell on deaf ears. Frankie dragged Pen down onto the floor and snatched a thick bushel of her hair. Then he cut it with the scissors.

Pen began to weep as strands of her soft brown hair fell to the carpet in front of her.

Less than ten minutes later, Frankie had hacked every last hair from Pen's head, leaving her bald. She looked like a different person now, face stained black with mascara. Andrew's heart hurt so badly that for a moment he thought he was having a heart attack.

Frankie was grinning. "She looks much hotter now, don't ya think?"

Andrew spat. "Fuck you!"

Frankie rushed forward and struck Andrew across his face. Stars invaded his vision and he wondered if the blow had broken his jaw. He moved it left and right, sparking extra pain.

"Come on, Frankie," said Davie. "You've made your point. They're both in tears. Let's go."

Frankie turned and pointed the scissors at Davie and shook his head. "I ain't even started yet, little bro."

"What did this guy do to you?" Davie asked.

Frankie's lip twitched as his anger seemed to rise. "Why do you care so much, man? He's just some stuck-up cunt with a flash car that thinks his shit don't stink."

Is that it? Andrew thought desperately. Is this whole thing just because I have a nice car? This whole nightmare is down to some insecure thug resenting me, jealous of what I have?

"What's your problem, D," asked Michelle. "Just chill your beans. You're acting like a prick."

"Hey," said Frankie, pointing the scissors at his girlfriend. "Don't talk to him like that. Davie's just sensitive. He don't mean no harm."

Davie nodded. "I just don't like any of this. It's going to end badly."

"Yeah, for him," said Dom, pointing at Andrew.

Andrew sat silently, bewildered by what was becoming some sort of surreal soap opera: people bickering casually in front of him whilst he was held captive in his own living room.

Davie helped Pen back onto the sofa, pulling her up by a handful of duct tape at her back. Then he sat back down beside her. For some reason, Davie was protective over Pen, and Andrew wondered if it stemmed from issues he had with his own mother.

Andrew turned his head to the floor as a noise alerted him. When he saw who was making it, he felt nauseous. Things were about to get worse.

Frankie looked down at Bex, who was now stirring on the floor, and grinned. "Well, lookey here. Little miss fine-ass is finally joining us. Now we can really step things up. Let's see how much of a party-girl she is, dad."

Andrew watched Frankie approach his daughter and, for the first time in his life, he prayed to God.

-13-

Andrew had never seen a person wake up screaming before, but that's just what Bex did. As soon as she regained consciousness, the agony of her broken wrist kicked in and she bellowed. Frankie marched forward and kicked her in the ribs, knocking loose every last ounce of breath she had in her lungs. "Keep it the fuck down!"

Bex's screams turned to inward gasping and the hissing sound she made was like the venting air brakes of a bus.

"Please," said Andrew. "Please, just leave my family alone. Do what you want to me..."

Frankie winked at Andrew as if they were old buddies. "I'm going to do that anyway, mate, so what exactly are you trying to negotiate with?"

"For God's sake, Frankie, have some decency. My family have done nothing to you."

Frankie strolled over to Andrew and perched himself on the armrest of the chair. "I say otherwise. People like you look down their noses at people like me; think you can treat us like dirt. Doesn't matter if it's you or your women, you all think you're better."

"We are better," Pen hissed from behind him.

Frankie clicked his fingers. "There, you see? You're wife thinks I'm a piece of shit."

Andrew huffed. "Can you blame her?"

"Maybe not," Frankie allowed, "but there's a war going on. Survival of the fittest. You might have your nice house and your Mercedes, but when it comes right down to it, you're weak. When it comes down to you and me, face to face, you're the one shitting himself – not me. I'm the one with the control."

"We're not cavemen, Frankie. Life isn't decided by who has the biggest club anymore."

"If prison taught me anything, it's that we're as much like cavemen as we've ever been."

Andrew looked at the boy – for that was all he was – and couldn't figure out what was going on behind those narrow, twitching eyes. Did he really believe he was vindicated in doing this? That he was just fighting a war against people like Andrew? A war against the middle-class. The more he listened to Frankie, the more he was sure the kid wasn't stupid, but something disturbed him all the way down to the core.

"Look," said Andrew. "I can help you. Whatever's made you this way, we can sort it out. There's no need for any of this."

Frankie's lips quivered, not because of his usual twitch, but because he looked like he might break into tears. "Really? You can help me?"

Andrew nodded.

Frankie released a sudden gout of laughter. "You fuckin' nonce. Is that what you say to little kids right before you snatch 'em up in your white van?" He drove a fist into Andrew's stomach and made him gasp, then leaned forward, closer. "You fuckin' pedo!"

Bex finally managed to catch her breath and started whining in pain again, writhing back and forth on the carpet. She was trying to keep her agony as quiet as possible, not wanting to draw any further reprisals from Frankie, but was failing badly. Andrew wished more than anything that he could help his daughter and take her pain unto him.

But he couldn't. Because an immoral thug wouldn't let him. Frankie had control over the welfare of them all now. Knowing that chilled Andrew to his bones.

The 10pm news came on the television and, for a moment, Andrew had the crazy notion that he would appear on it. Family man found dead in home. Wife and daughter murdered. His skin seemed to vibrate at the thought, the fear and panic threatening to burst through his skin. He needed to get free. He needed to save his family.

Frankie grabbed Rebecca by the hair and hoisted her up to her feet, then examined her up and down. She was wearing her nightdress and was totally bare from just above the knee downwards. Andrew wished she'd listened to him about covering up.

"You going to give the bitch a haircut like her old lady?" Michelle asked, thick dollops of spite in her voice. Andrew bet the girl was jealous of his daughter. In a beauty contest, Bex would win handsdown. In a situation like this, however, her beauty could be a danger. There were few things nastier than a jealous girl.

"Come on," Michelle urged. "Shave the slut."

Frankie shook his head. "Be quiet, Shell. I make the decisions here." He turned Bex to face him and smiled at her almost tenderly. "What's your name, sweetheart?"

"Rebecca."

"Okay, Rebecca. I'm going to do you a favour because you're so goddamn fine. If you promise to sit by your mom and behave, I won't hurt you or even tape you up. Agreed?"

Bex whimpered slightly, likely due to the pain she was in, but managed to nod and say, "Yes."

"Good girl." Frankie kissed her on the cheek and pushed her down on the sofa. "Davie, you watch the both of 'em, okay? No fucks ups, you get me?"

Michelle screeched. "What? You're just going to leave her alone? Why?"

"Because that's what I decided to do," said Frankie. "Now shut the hell up before I bounce your ass."

Michelle shut up but did not look happy. Andrew sat and enjoyed the relief that Bex might not be in any immediate danger. Frankie's apparent attraction to her had ensured her safety for now. He just hope that attraction didn't lead to something worse.

"So what we going to do instead, Frankie?" Jordan asked.

"We're going to do some more blow. Except I don't want to do it on that coffee table anymore. It looks dirty."

"Where then?" Dom asked.

"Grab the old lady."

Dom and Jordan looked at each other and shrugged, seeming not to understand the request but happy to follow it all the same. They headed over to the sofa and grabbed one of Pen's arms each, before lifting her to her feet.

"Now what?" asked Dom.

Frankie smirked. He picked up the scissors from the coffee table and waved them back and forth in front of his face. Andrew held his breath and waited for whatever fate was about to befall his wife. He wanted to close his eyes but couldn't. He owed Pen more than that.

Frankie thrust the scissors at Pen, but didn't stab her. Instead he began cutting her blouse through the middle, starting at the neckline. She didn't struggle, her fight was gone and her face lacked expression. The bindings around her wrists made escape impossible. It didn't take long for Frankie to cut the blouse free, letting it fall to the floor in tatters. Pen stood there rigidly, topless except for her purple-cotton bra – Andrew's favourite.

"Lay her across the table," said Frankie. "Face up."

It was then that Pen found her instincts – struggling to break free of her captors and lashing out with the only weapon she had: her teeth. Dom hollered in pain as she bit him and leapt back. He slapped her across the face. "Fuckin' bitch!"

The twins forced Pen down onto the table and held her there, arms above her head so that her midriff was exposed.

"Leave her alone," Andrew screamed. "Leave her alone, leave her alone, leave her alone!"

Frankie leapt across the room and punched Andrew in his nose, spreading it across his face and unleashing a torrent of blood. Then he grabbed the tape and wrapped several layers around Andrew's head, covering his mouth – and almost, too, his nose. Through teary eyes, he was forced to watch and breathe through his damaged sinuses.

Frankie went back to Pen, pulled a baggie from his pocket and bit a hole into it. Then he upturned it and sprinkled the contents onto her exposed stomach. It was more cocaine. Frankie used the edge of the kitchen scissors to separate the pile into several messy lines on Pen's stomach.

"Dig in, gangsters."

Andrew watched helplessly as the teenagers took turns snorting coke from his wife's belly, holding her down by the feet and wrists to keep her from squirming. After a while she just gave up struggling all together and let them have their way.

-14-

Almost unbelievably, Frankie, the twins, and Michelle had all sat down in a huddle on the carpet to watch television. Davie remained on the sofa, watching over the women like he'd been told to. Unlike the others, he'd not snorted any coke and was completely sober. Watching them now, half-passed out on the floor and transfixed by a documentary about increasing climate change, he was glad about that.

Davie did drugs sometimes, just weed mostly, but he had always stayed away from the hard stuff. Fortunately, Frankie never tried to force it on him; otherwise he would probably have been persuaded by now. Even his mother did it during the times when she and Frankie got on.

"Let us go," Rebecca said.

Davie looked at her and got caught in the stare of her soulful dark eyes.

"I said, let us go. Please."

Davie shook his head. "I can't. You'll get my brother into trouble."

Rebecca huffed. "He's already in trouble. Kidnap is serious."

"He hasn't kidnapped anyone. You're still at home."

"It's still kidnap. He's holding us hostage. Davie, please."

Hearing her say his name sent a shiver down his spine. Girls like Rebecca didn't usually talk to him, let alone speak his name. Skanks like

Michelle were more the type of girl he was used to being around. He shook his head once more, but this time tried to express how much he regretted the situation. He wanted her to know that if it were up to him, none of this would be happening. "I hate all this," he said. "I really do, but Frankie's my brother. Family comes first."

"What about my family? Do they mean nothing? Innocent people who never hurt anybody."

Davie shrugged. It seemed there was no right answer he could give. Frankie was his brother and that was that. He would trust him as he had always done. Things would work out somehow. They had to.

"Look what they've done to my mother," Rebecca kept on.

Davie looked to his right and examined the woman. She was sprawled back on the sofa, staring at the ceiling and almost never blinking. She had a dusty film of cocaine particles all over her naked bod and thicker clumps of it clung to the fabric of her bra. Davie tried not to stare at her large, round breasts.

"Do you know that she's a special needs worker?" Rebecca said. "She teaches kids from broken homes, just like you. She tries to help people just like you."

Davie knew the role of special needs teachers – he'd dealt with many – and could agree that they were generally very kind people, but none of them ever did any good. Kids like him and his brother never had a chance of anything aside from turning out just like their deadbeat parents. In fact, special needs teachers succeeded only in giving false hope. Davie didn't waste his time with such things.

"Be quiet," he said. "I don't want to hear it."

"Fine," Rebecca conceded, "but by doing nothing, you're just as bad as they are."

Was it true? thought Davie. Am I...bad?

He scanned the room, observing his brother and girlfriend as they kissed and groped each other on the floor. Then he watched Dom and Jordan, scratching at their balls and laughing at a television program that was not trying to be funny. Finally, he looked back at Andrew, who looked right back at him, eyes swollen half-shut either side of a crumpled nose.

I'm not bad, he told himself. I'm not like Frankie...but I'm not good either, am I? Or maybe I'm just weak...

Davie stared at the television and tried not to think anymore. He had a feeling that the truth would hurt him.

-15-

Horror melded with disgust inside Andrew's stomach as the teenagers cavorted on his floor. Under the influence of grade-A drugs, Frankie's lack of inhibitions persuaded him to pull off Michelle's jeans and tug aside her skimpy thong. He then proceeded to enter the moaning girl, right there on the carpet, rutting like monkeys on the Discovery Channel.

How could anyone be so decadent? Frankie truly had no conception of other people's feelings at all. It was almost like the world was just an illusion that revolved around his desires.

Andrew turned his head away as Frankie began to climax, his naked buttocks clenching as he ejaculated for what seemed like forever. Dom and Jordan lay watching television as if they didn't notice.

"You disgust me," said Bex from the sofa, far braver than her father for being the one to speak out.

Frankie pulled his dick out of Michelle and a sloppy, wet sound emanated from between them. He stood up and fastened his jeans, then laughed right in Bex's face while grabbing his crotch. "Just jealous because you want a piece of this too. Don't worry, sweetheart, maybe later."

"Never going to happen," she said. "I'd rather fuck a pig."

Frankie's joking demeanour suddenly soured. "You show me some fucking respect or I'll forget all about my earlier offer of leaving you in one piece."

Bex chose to say nothing and Andrew was relieved about it. If she just kept her mouth closed then perhaps the only one to suffer tonight would be him. The ironic thing was that watching his daughter's torment hurt Andrew more than anything Frankie could ever do to him directly. By staying quiet, Bex would be doing everyone a favour.

Frankie looked at Andrew and then motioned to Pen on the sofa. She was in some sort of unbroken daze, fixated on an invisible spot on the ceiling. "I think she's lost the plot, mate? She this lively in bed?"

Andrew laughed a bitter laugh. "You're evil. Hell would be too good for you."

"Maybe they'll make a place just for me, then. Some deep dark abyss where I don't have to put up with pricks like you."

Andrew's eyebrows rose. "I'm the prick. That's a good one."

"You getting lippy with me, mate? I already broke your nose; want me to break something else?"

Andrew shook his head, but still couldn't keep a lid on his anger. "Go right ahead. What difference is it going to make?"

Frankie grinned as if he knew something that no one else did. Without warning, he turned and punched Pen in her ribs. She cried out in shock and pain before crumpling to the floor and gasping. Frankie held his fist up to Andrew and winked at him. "You piss me off, I'll take it out on her."

Andrew didn't speak. He was in Hell; a hell where he could do nothing but watch the people he loved suffer.

Maybe that's what Hell was? Not being punished yourself, but having to watch others suffer for your sins.

"Do we fuckin' understand one another?" Frankie snarled.

Andrew nodded.

Frankie clapped his hands together. "Good. Now get up and fight me."

Andrew blinked. "What?"

Frankie raised both fists in a boxer's pose. "I want to see what you got, old man."

Andrew was confused. "I'm tied up."

"I know that, you fuckin' mug. Dom will let you loose, innit."

Dom heard his name and looked up from the television, fuzzy-eyed and half asleep.

Andrew thought about things for a second and decided this could be his chance. The only opportunity he might have of getting away and reaching help. He had to take it, even though he was frightened enough to piss himself.

"Okay, Frankie. I'll fight you."

Frankie started throwing punches into the air, fighting an opponent only he could see. "Cool. Dom, get him loose. Use the scissors – but keep a hold of em."

Lest I drive them into your skull, thought Andrew. Adrenaline had already begun coursing through his veins in anticipation. Fighting was a skill far beyond him and he had no doubt that Frankie would beat him in short order, but standing toe-to-toe with the barbaric thug was not a plan he intended to follow. He had other ideas.

Dom hacked away at the duct tape roped around Andrew's body. With each passing second, Andrew felt the bonds loosen and the circulation return to his arms. Several minutes later and Andrew was finally free. He stood up and winced as the pressure in his kneecaps caused them to click painfully.

Frankie stood in front of him and clenched both hands into fists, holding them aloft his chin like a boxer. "What shall we say? Three-minute rounds? Or shall we just fight till a knockout?"

Andrew took the opportunity to, one last time, try and reason with his attacker. "You don't have to do this, Frankie. You can just leave right now. No one blames you for any of this. Your mother has obviously failed you."

The comment seemed to strike a chord with Frankie and his clenched fists lowered slightly. He spat onto the carpet. "Bitch has nothing to do with me."

Andrew nodded. "I know, and that's a shame. No one deserves to be raised like that."

"You don't know shit! Not a thing, so don't play the caring soul with me. People like you couldn't give two shits about people like us."

"Yeah," said Michelle. "Just put his lights out, Frankie, and be done with it."

Frankie nodded over to his girlfriend and raised his fists again. Then he rang an imaginary bell. "Ding! Ding!"

With Frankie approaching, ready to strike like a viper, Andrew made his own move. He dashed for the living room door.

"The fuckers trying to do one," said Jordan from the floor.

Andrew shoved through the door and barrelled into the hallway. He turned to his right and sprinted for the porch. His plan was to rush into the street and cry out for help. His neighbours might not come, but at least one of them would surely call the police.

But when he reached the porch, the front door was locked.

"Looking for these?" asked Frankie, jangling a set of keys in his hand and standing in the living room doorway.

Andrew was cornered. He looked about himself and snatched at the first thing he could find, which happened to be a golfing brolly. He hopped forwards, holding the folded umbrella in front of him like a spear.

Frankie sniggered. "The fuck you going to do with that? Catch the blood that's going to be raining down when I catch you?"

Andrew considered the viability of his weapon and realised it was nowhere near enough to win a fight with the youths. He had to run – but to where?

He eyed the stairs.

"Don't even think about it," Frankie warned.

With panic threatening to explode his heart, Andrew made a break for it. Frankie snatched out at him with both arms, but Andrew managed to fend him off by poking the umbrella into his face. The sharp point found its mark and caused Frankie to flinch back against the wall, clutching his eye.

"Fuckin' dead man. I'm going to mess you up."

Andrew ignored the hateful comments and raced up the stairs, taking the steps two at a time. Frankie shouted commands, rallying his drug-addled troops into battle. There was the sound of them funnelling into the downstairs hallway.

Andrew sped across the landing and headed for the only room he knew that had a lock: the bathroom. Once inside, he slammed the door shut and turned the catch. Then he quickly dragged the linen basket across the tiled floor and placed it in front of the door to form a barricade. He collapsed on top of it, huffing and puffing like he'd just run a marathon. It was all going to be for nothing, though. The door was too thin to hold out for long and, upon realising that, Andrew understood his big mistake.

He had trapped himself.

In any other room of the house he might have escaped through one of the windows, or at least cried out for help, but the bathroom had only a slim, horizontal pane of frosted glass set high into the wall. Even if he broke the glass it was too small to get through.

It wasn't long before Frankie arrived and started to kick the door in.

***

"You're a dead man!" Frankie thrust another kick at the door.

The flimsy wood at Andrew's back had already begun to crack, and weakened further with every blow. He pushed back against the door, trying to it brace it, but it was no good. Frankie was going to get through eventually.

Andrew checked out his surroundings in a bathroom that suddenly seemed very alien to him. It had once been a room where he would relax, de-stress, and release the worries of his day – but no more. Now it was a cage and he was the rat trapped inside of it.

Another kick and the door rattled inside the fragile woodwork of the frame. He fell away from the door and began rifling through the wall cabinets. He found nothing with which to defend himself. The recently-renovated room was a jewel of modernist design – which meant it was empty. He put his hands on the only thing that seemed even slightly dangerous and pulled at it. The chrome towel rail came away from the wall easily, the thin cavity wall offering no resistance. The quality of newer built homes did not compare to the industrious design of Victorian housing, but Andrew was thankful for that right now. However, it was also the reason that a large, cracking dent was widening in the middle of the bathroom's flimsy door.

Andrew prepared himself.

"You're finished, mate," Frankie shouted through the door, rage filling his voice like boiling liquid into a beaker. "I'm going to kill your wife then hold you down and drown you in her blood"

"Yeah," said a female voice that could only have been Michelle. "But I'm going to stamp on your head first, you fuckin' perv!"

Andrew could hear Dom and Jordan out on the landing as well, could hear their sniggering. A desperate anger started to fill him – a sudden spark of insanity that affected him to the point of wild madness. He clutched the towel rail above his head and told himself it was a mighty broadsword. He pictured his attackers as pillaging Vikings coming to take his land and women.

Frankie continued kicking at the door.

The wood splintered.

Cracked.

Caved.

Frankie gave one last, hefty kick that splintered the frame and broke the lock. The door swung open slowly, linen basket sliding out of the way easily.

Frankie poked his head through the gap and grinned maniacally. "Hey man, what you up to? Guy spends too long in the bathroom it starts to look a little... unsavoury."

Andrew huffed defiantly, still clutching the towel rail above his head. "Nice word. You learn that today? Here's another one for you – Pussy!"

Frankie broke into the bathroom.

Andrew swung the towel rail.

The blow connected and Frankie stumbled backwards, lost his balance as the backs of his legs hit the lip of the room's bathtub and sent him tumbling into it. There was a loud crack as the back of the boy's skull hit the enamel.

Andrew took advantage of the situation. As Frankie struggled to get out of the tub, he made a run for it. But Jordan and Dom blocked his way. Before they had chance to grab him, Andrew swung the towel rail again. The blow missed both targets and hit the battered frame of the doorway, but it was enough to make the two boys flinch and step back. Andrew suddenly found himself facing an open doorway.

He was just about to race out into the hallway when something bit into his calf, producing a white-hot jolt that seemed to travel up his entire leg.

Andrew fell down onto his knees.

Frankie appeared, standing over Andrew and grinning. He ran his tongue along the edge of a knife he was holding in his hand, licking away a sheen of blood.

"What are we going to do with you, Andrew?"

Andrew didn't get chance to answer. Frankie lifted up his foot and stamped on his head.

-16-

Davie sat in the living room listening to the ruckus upstairs. The women sat beside him and shuddered with every sound.

"It will be okay," Davie told them. "They'll all be gone soon. My brother's just having a laugh."

Rebecca looked at him like he was an idiot. "A laugh? Are you insane? Someone is going to end up dead and you'll be just as much to blame as your psycho brother."

Davie shook his head. "I haven't done anything wrong."

"Wake up, you idiot. Your brother's dragged you into this. You're the one keeping an eye on us – that makes you one of the kidnappers. You'll rot in jail unless you let us go right now."

Davie wanted to make her see sense, but managed only to choke on a mouthful of words that never managed to form into sentences.

"You're in a mess and you know it," Rebecca stated. "You don't want any of this, do you? You don't want to end up a worthless thug like your brother."

"Shut up," Davie told her. "I won't hear you talk like that about Frankie."

She shook her head at him in a way he did not like. "Stop defending him, Davie. You're not like him, I can tell. You're a good person."

Davie ran both hands through his hair and let out a long breath. His head still ached and now he felt dizzy as well. The banging and shouting from upstairs didn't help the situation. How did things get so crazy? Did it start when he was hit by Andrew's car, or was this whole turn of events inevitable even before that? He had a feeling that Andrew and Frankie were destined to reach this point regardless. He just hoped his involvement hadn't made things worse.

"Let us go," Rebecca said calmly. "This is the point where you decide whether you want to be part of this or not. If you let us go now, then it'll be clear that you just got caught up in something accidentally. Keep us here, though, and you're proving that you're as happy to go along with this as the others."

Davie stared down at the carpet, down at a chunk of browning fish meat that jutted out from beneath the sofa. He thought about things long and hard before he eventually looked Rebecca in the eye. "He'll kill me if I help you. You'll have him arrested and when he gets out he will literally kill me. Frankie is all I have so why would I want to make him hate me?"

Rebecca stared back at him with her deep, dark eyes. "Because you know that this is wrong, Davie."

Davie nodded. He didn't want to see this girl get hurt – in fact he couldn't bear it. "Okay," he said, regretting already what he was about to do, yet powerless to stop himself from doing it. "Get out of here, quick."

Rebecca put her arms around Davie and squeezed him tightly. "Thank you," she whispered into his ear, then stood up and grabbed her mother's limp hand. "Come on, mum. We can go and get help now. It's all over."

Davie knew the decision he'd just made was the right one – could tell by the love and concern Rebecca had for her mother – but it didn't make him feel any less apprehensive. Frankie was definitely going to kill him.

Rebecca managed to get her mother standing, despite the woman's hands and feet being bound, and was now looking down at Davie with an expression he wasn't used to. It looked like compassion. "I'll make sure the police know that you had nothing to do with this. You should get out of here, too, before Frankie comes back dow-"

Andrew crashed through the living room door and sprawled onto the carpet beside the sofa. His hands were covered in blood, as were his jeans and shirt. Frankie came through the door after him, followed by the others. He kicked Andrew in the stomach before he had a chance to get up. Andrew was silent as the blow crushed his ribs and sent him reeling onto his back. Covered by blood and swollen in the face, he looked more dead than alive.

Frankie looked around and noticed that the women were now standing. Davie swallowed a lump in his throat as he waited for his brother's reaction.

"Sit down, bitches," Frankie ordered.

Rebecca did not sit down as instructed and instead lunged right at Frankie with her fingernails pointed out like claws. There was a deep-red lump already growing on his forehead and Rebecca added to it by gouging two long furrows into the flesh of his cheek. The scratches began to bleed instantly, but Frankie reacted quickly. He punched Rebecca hard in her stomach and doubled her over in agony, then he pushed her by the head down to the ground. He made it look as effortless as discarding trash.

"Tie this slag up," he ordered the twins before looking at Davie and scowling. "What the fuck, man? You were meant to be keeping these two under control."

Davie nodded. "I'm sorry. I was distracted when you all burst in. Sorry."

Frankie let his expression soften and walked over to his brother. Wrapping his hand around Davie's head, he pulled him close, forehead touching forehead. "Don't sweat it, little bro. No harm done. You just keep watching my back like you always do and nothing will ever hurt me. You're my good-luck charm."

Davie hoped that wasn't true, but was glad that his brother was not angry with him. He decided it best to try and help get things back under control again. Any chance that the women had of escaping was now gone and there was no point working against his brother now. It was over.

Penelope was still standing aimlessly so Davie eased her back down onto the sofa, then knelt down beside Rebecca on the floor. She was lying on her side, breathing in and out rapidly and wincing in pain. Davie waited a few moments until she managed to catch her breath. Then he stroked her back and said, "Let's get back on the sofa. If you're quiet, Frankie might leave you alone."

Rebecca said nothing, but she rolled herself up onto her knees and climbed back on the sofa. Her breathing was still awkward.

Dom and Jordan came over with the duct tape. "Get her to her feet, Davie."

"She'll be okay, lads. I'll make sure she behaves."

Dom shook his head. "Get her on her fucking feet, Davie. You heard your brother. He said, tie the slag up."

Davie glanced at Rebecca who was looking back at him sadly. He couldn't tell for sure, but something about the way she looked at him told him that she at least now understood that he had no choice in the matter. He had tried, at least.

He reached forward and pulled Rebecca's feet onto his lap. They were small, dainty, with perfect little toes painted a deep purple. He had to force himself not to gaze further up her naked legs and beneath her nightgown. He knew little about women, but he knew not to stare.

Dom got to work, wrapping the silver duct tape around Rebecca's ankles so tight that it made her wince. She did not complain, though. After he was done with her legs, Dom had Davie grab her wrists while he trussed them up as well.

"Do the bitch's mouth," said Frankie from the other side of the room. He was busy getting an unconscious Andrew back into the armchair and Michelle was helping him.

"No worries," said Dom, happily tearing off another thick wad of tape and stamping it over Rebecca's mouth. Jordan came forward to join his brother and squeezed one of her breasts. She tried to cry out in pain but could only mumble from behind the tape.

"Don't worry," Jordan said. "We'll take the tape off later when we have a use for your mouth."

Davie wanted to slap Jordan for saying such a horrid thing to a frightened girl, but he knew that he would just take a clobbering. He couldn't take Dom or Jordan on his best day and their worst – and especially not with a concussion and a stomach that kept threatening to empty itself.

"Okay," said Frankie, clapping his hands together. "Everybody nice and settled again?"

No one said anything, but all turned in his direction.

"Then I think this would be a good time to explain to everyone what happens when people don't follow my rules." He turned to Andrew and slapped his cheeks hard. "Stay with us, hero. I was about to tell your bitches what a fine display you put on up there."

"What happened?" Davie asked, knowing that the answer wouldn't be anything good.

"What happened, little bro, is that this gangster right here took a pole to my skull. Fair play, I say, but it never did him no good in the end. My knife was mightier than his pole."

Rebecca moaned beneath the tape on her mouth and Davie matched her reaction by stretching his eyes wide. "You stabbed him?"

Frankie shrugged. "Had no choice. Guy was out of control and needed putting down."

"We need to go, Frankie. This is getting bad."

"Shut the hell up, Davie," said Michelle from Frankie's side. "You're such a downer all the time."

Usually, Frankie would jump to his brother's defence, but this time he didn't, which Davie took as a bad sign. "Okay," he said, not wanting to anger his brother. "What now then?"

Frankie smirked. "Glad you asked. What we're going to do now is show Andrew the error of his ways. Man took a chunk out of my forehead. He needs to pay for that."

"You already stabbed him," said Davie.

Frankie nodded. "That was just to detain him. If the police catch you and give you a kicking you still go to court afterwards. They don't take the beating required to subdue you as the punishment for the crime."

"Yeah," said Dom. "He still needs to be put on trial."

"And so here we are," said Frankie, gushing with amusement, "to pre-side over the people versus Mr Andrew...whatever the fuck his name is."

"Goodman," Davie muttered.

"What are the charges," asked Michelle, happily playing along with the charade.

"Kiddie-fiddling, goat-fucking, and the crime of thinking his shit don't stink."

"How do you find?" asked Jordan, laughing till he was out of breath.

Frankie held a finger in the air to silence the room. He seemed deep in thought, but then suddenly thrust his finger at the floor and screamed the word, "GUILTY!"

"What is his punishment?" asked Dom gleefully.

Frankie put his hands together and placed his fingertips beneath his nose as if trying to gain guidance from God himself. "Through the power invested in me by the courts, I sentence this wicked man to a slow and lingering death...by torture."

Torture – Davie repeated the word in his head three times. Then he threw up.

-17-

"You okay, man?" Frankie had moved over to rub Davie's back while he continued to be sick.

Davie spat a wad of saliva onto the carpet and wiped his mouth with the back of his hand. "I think so. Just came over me all of a sudden."

"Must be the concussion," Frankie suggested. "Don't worry. He's going to pay for what he did to you."

Davie shook his head and looked up at his brother pleadingly. "I just want to go home. I feel rough, man. Need to go to bed."

Frankie examined him for several seconds then nodded. "Okay, Davie. We'll get you home to rest."

"Really?"

"Yeah." Frankie smiled at him warmly. "Just as soon as I'm done here. Let me finish up."

Davie took some deep breaths and tried to calm his stomach before he spoke. "Finish up?"

Frankie leant closer and whispered in Davie's ear. "Got to get rid of the witnesses."

"No way," said Davie. "You can't be serious." He leant forward and lowered his voice so that only Frankie could hear the question he was about to ask. "You're not really going to kill anybody, are you?"

Frankie looked at Davie and nodded very slowly, very seriously. The cold cubes of ice that were his eyes chilled Davie to the bone. He finally realised that he no longer knew the person standing in front of him. Something had changed inside of Frankie when he went to prison. He'd come back a monster. What the hell had happened to him in that young offender's home?

"I don't want to kill anybody," said Davie, tears forming in his eyes.

"You don't have to, little bro. Leave it all up to big brother. Haven't I always looked after you?"

Davie nodded. The urge to vomit was rising up from his guts again and he fought hard to contain it.

"This is getting boring, Frankie. Let's fuck something up." It was Michelle. The sound of her voice was like a squealing pig to Davie's ears. If someone really was about to die, he wished it would be her.

His upper lip curled up in a snarl. "Shut the hell up, Shell, you coked-up whore."

Michelle marched forward and grabbed a hold of Frankie's arm. "You going to let the little wanker talk to me like that?"

Frankie shrugged away from her grasp and turned to Davie. He let out a short laugh but looked deadly serious. "You got to learn to play nice, little bro. That was out of line, you get me?"

"Is that it?" said Michelle, stamping her feet and waving her arms like an outraged child.

Frankie slapped her across the face. It wasn't hard enough to injure her but had enough force to knock her to the ground. "How many fucking times have I told you to leave it out, you skinny cunt?"

Michelle fell to the floor and cowered, raising her arms up to deflect any further blows. "I...I'm sorry, baby. Please..."

Frankie clicked his fingers at her. "Get the fuck up and be quiet. You give my brother shit one more time and I'll end you."

Michelle nodded and hurried away to the far side of the room. Davie noticed that Dom and Jordan were sat watching the television again but were keeping one eye on the argument and giggling between themselves.

Davie shook his head. You're all just a bunch of crack heads.

"Okay," Frankie rubbed his hands together. "It's getting cold in here so I'm going to go and put the heating on. When I get back it will be time to carry out sentencing. Dom, Jordan, sort your shit out and wake up. You're sat watching the snooker championships and giggling your arses off like it's the funniest thing you ever saw."

Dom and Jordan suddenly looked like naughty children and hurried to their feet quickly. Frankie left the room and Michelle ran after him, no doubt to fawn over him and try to make up. Davie sat down on the sofa between the women and worried about their fates. Penelope was still staring into space. Rebecca had let her head drop.

A garbled murmur let those in the room know that Andrew had regained consciousness. He was looking across the room at Davie through his swollen eyelids.

"Everything will be okay," Davie told him, hating himself for lying. "We're all going soon."

"Yeah," said Dom, "after we deal with your pasty, white ass."

"Why...why do you follow him?" Andrew asked the room. Davie wasn't sure who it was directed at, but he figured it was a valid question to each of them.

"We don't follow no one," said Jordan. "We just hang with Frankie cus he's got the supply."

"So you...help him terrorise innocent people just because he feeds you drugs?"

"That about sums it up, blud." Jordan couldn't help himself but laugh. "Sucks for you, huh, whitey?"

Andrew laughed, too – it was a thick, throaty sound, full of derision and disdain. "I think it sucks for you...that you let another man own your ass. You're just Frankie's bitches." He broke out in even harder laughter; despite the obvious difficulty he had taking in air through his crumpled nose. Dom and Jordan were furious, but also lost for words. It wasn't very often anyone had the balls to sound off at them like that. Davie looked down at the floor and grinned.

Frankie re-entered the room carrying a tea towel that seemed to be wrapped around something. He moved to the centre of the room and placed the tea towel on the coffee table, before unravelling it to reveal a set of variously-sized knives, a corkscrew, screwdriver, and a pair of pliers.

"What are those for?" asked Davie, already knowing the answer.

Frankie sighed at his brother. "Enough with the questions. You're giving me such a headache that I might end up being the one with concussion."

Dom came over and looked down at the assorted implements. He whistled. "Shit's gunna get real, huh?"

Frankie picked up a small steel knife and examined the edge with the pad of his thumb. When he was satisfied with its sharpness, he sauntered over towards Andrew, waving it back and forth.

"You ready for sentencing, old man?"

Andrew lifted his head and looked Frankie in the eye. There was no fear in his expression anymore; only a weariness that could have been acceptance. Davie held his breath as he waited for what was to come.

Frankie pointed the knife in Andrew's face. "Swallowed your fucking tongue?"

Andrew spat then; a mixture of blood and saliva that hit Frankie right in his face.

Frankie's twitch went into overdrive as his face screwed up in fury. It suddenly occurred to Davie that his brother had not possessed a facial tick before he'd gone away.

Frankie placed the blade against the flesh below Andrew's left eye. "You going to wish you never did that, gangster."

"I don't give a fuck," said Andrew calmly, but his breathing was beginning to quicken and his voice was slightly unsteady.

Frankie smiled. "We going to see how much of a fuck you don't give, old man." He removed the knife from Andrew's face, turned around, and shuffled over to the sofa so that he was standing behind Penelope. "You positive I can't make you care?"

Andrew's swollen eyes flinched. "Don't!"

"Don't what?" said Frankie. "Don't do this?"

Frankie drew the blade across the side of Penelope's face, drawing a slick line of blood as he flayed open the flesh of her cheek. At first she made no sound, still trapped in whatever daze had imprisoned her, but then she snapped back to reality and let out a high-pitched wail that could have cracked crystal. Frankie wrapped a hand around her mouth and stifled her.

From beside Davie, Rebecca struggled to get free. He had to put both hands on her to keep her in place. He wasn't trying to help Frankie; he was trying to help her.

"Thought you didn't give a fuck?" said Frankie to Andrew as he etched another long slice across his wife's face. "Looks like you care now."

No one said anything, the air tense enough to carry electric. Frankie continued to gag Penelope with his hand for several more minutes, finally letting go when her sobbing and moaning quieted down. She shook and trembled as he released her.

Frankie cricked his neck to the side and shuddered. "Damn, that was fun."

"You sick fuck," Andrew cursed him. "You sick sick fuck!"

"Those cuts are deep, bro," said Dom. "They ain't never gunna heal right. Scarred for life, yo."

Davie agreed. The cuts were thick and blood rolled down both sides of Penelope's face. Along with her bald head, and the other abuses of the night, Davie knew that the deepest scares would be the ones inside her mind. Frankie had caused damage that no amount of therapy would ever cure.

"Can I cut someone now?" Michelle asked almost innocently. As if she was an eight-year old asking to taste her daddy's wine.

Frankie offered out the knife. "Sure thing, sweetie."

Michelle took the knife and immediately headed for Rebecca.

Frankie put a hand out and stopped her. "Not so fast, baby girl. No one touches the women but me."

Michelle's entire face drooped. "Seriously? Come on. Just let me cut her a little bit. Slapper thinks she's the shit. Needs bringing down a peg."

Frankie didn't speak. He just stared at Michelle, unblinking.

"Okay, okay," she relented. "I'll slice her dad then."

She took the knife over to Andrew who looked back at her defiantly. "How did a nice girl like Charlie ever have a friend like you?" he asked.

Michelle hissed at him. "I kicked that bitch to the curb long time ago. Thought she was better than me."

"That's because she is."

Michelle lashed out with the knife, hitting against Andrew's ribs with an audible clink. The knife was small and could only have entered an inch or so, but it was more than enough to make Andrew bellow in pain.

Davie covered his ears.

"Hey," Frankie shouted. "Watch where you're cutting. You'll end up killing him."

Davie sat up straight, buoyed by his big brother's comment. Maybe he didn't want to kill anyone after all. Why else would he have just told Shell to be careful?

"Isn't that what you want?" Michelle asked Frankie.

"No," he replied. "Not yet, at least. Got to make him feel it first."

Davie sighed. The brief glimmer of hope he'd felt faded away. This couldn't go on any longer, surely? What more damage could Frankie do? Penelope would never be the same again and most likely neither would Andrew – if he lived. Rebecca still had a chance, though. She could still get through this in one piece if it all ended now. Davie closed his eyes, took a deep breath, and made a decision. It was time he stood up to his big brother. This had to stop now.

-18-

Andrew was afraid, he could not deny that, but there was strength inside him now that he'd never known existed before. The pain he'd experienced, and was still yet to experience, was not enough to break him – in fact it had only made his resolve stronger. He wouldn't beg, he would not plead. The hell Frankie put him through had changed something in him. He had seen into the depth of his own physical being – the deepness of his soul – and knew now that he would never stop fighting for his family.

But things had changed when Frankie slashed Pen's face. The pain of seeing his wife's beautiful face disfigured found a way past his barriers and struck right at his heart. A pressure grew inside his chest that threatened to explode his very being. As quickly as it had arrived, the fight fled out of him.

Frankie approached with a new weapon – one he hadn't yet used to torture anyone. He held the pliers at arm's length and snapped them shut menacingly. "Time for your dental appointment, sir."

Andrew sighed and let his head drop to his chest, mentally preparing himself for another helping of agony. He sent his mind to a meditative place of calm indifference that offered a sliver of emotionally sanctuary. It was a place inside of himself that he'd not known existed before this night. Pain and suffering had forced it into existence, rending itself into his psyche out of necessity and survival.

"I've never done a root canal before," said Frankie, "but I'm sure it'll go alright. What do you think?"

Andrew said nothing. If he did then the animal might hurt his family some more. Whatever happened, he could take it – or at least tolerate – as long as it was done only to him.

Frankie grabbed Andrew's lower jaw with his grubby fingers and yanked it open. "Dear, oh, dear. That's some very bad tooth decay you have there. I think we're going to have to get those teeth out ASAP. Every single one of them."

The twins and Michelle gave a cheer to that as if it was the most exciting thing they had ever heard of. Andrew wondered if it was the drugs that made them this way, or if they'd been born wicked. They weren't human beings, they were baying dogs – hyenas.

Frankie shushed everyone into silence and started his procedure. Andrew spluttered and coughed as the pliers entered his mouth. They scratched against his tongue and clinked against his teeth, sending aching shudders down to their roots. Suddenly, the steel tongs clamped down on either side of a molar and Andrew felt the tooth crack beneath the sudden pressure. Agony exploded thorough his lower jaw and gradually travelled upwards to consume his entire face. His vision blurred as the pliers twisted side to side, yanking and wrenching the tooth away from the gum, millimetre by excruciating millimetre. Despite coming extremely near, Andrew didn't lose consciousness. He was still awake to see Frankie make a successful extraction and hold the retrieved molar in front of his audience like a grizzly trophy.

Andrew's mouth filled with hot, salty blood, so much that he thought he might choke on it. He spat endlessly to keep his mouth clear and the sight of all the blood seemed to cause a massive grin to stretch across Frankie's twitching face.

"That shit is gross," said Dom from a couple of meters away. "I could puke."

"Pull another one," Michelle screeched. "Do another before he passes out."

Frankie took the molar from the pliers and examined it between his fingers. He showed it to Andrew, too, waving it a couple of inches in front of his nose. "Mind if I keep this?"

The question disturbed Andrew. It was the type of thing a serial killer would do, keeping a memento from his victim's body. The notion of dying tonight was becoming more and more a reality to Andrew, but so was something else. If Frankie was going to kill him, he wouldn't stop there – couldn't stop there. Pen and Bex were witnesses that this monster could not afford to keep around. If

Andrew didn't get free, Frankie was going to kill his family.

"Time for the next tooth," said Frankie clicking the pliers open and shut. Blood still dripped from the implement.

"STOP IT!"

Andrew leant sideways and glanced around Frankie. What he saw was Davie, standing up beside the sofa and facing down his brother.

Frankie shook his head. "What the fuck, Davie?"

Davie's eyes narrowed beneath the bandage around his forehead. His slim shoulders were rigid, tense. "I'm done with this, Frankie. You've hurt these people enough and I can't take any more of this."

Andrew couldn't see Frankie's face now his back was turned, but he could tell by the unmoving body language that he was dumbfounded by his little brother's sudden outburst.

"What's your problem? This goddamn pedo ran you the fuck over."

"It was an accident," Davie shouted a decibel below a shout, "and it happened because I was running away after what you did to that girl at the chip shop. If you hadn't taken me along I wouldn't have got hit by no car."

"You keep your mouth shut about that. You want me to get pinched?"

Davie shook his head, exasperated. "You're already going to get pinched. You're planning on killing people."

"So what?" said Frankie. "Shit happens. Long as we're smart, no one will pin a thing on us."

Davie seemed incredulous. "Us? Us? I want nothing to do with this fucking mess. This is all down to you and your shit-faced mates."

"Hey man, that's not cool," said Jordan from the floor.

"No," Frankie agreed. "Not cool at all." He walked forward and prodded a finger into Davie's chest. "Now you chill the fuck out, little bro, or things are going to end bad for you."

Davie didn't move an inch. "I love you, Frankie, but if you carry on hurting these people, I ain't your bro no more."

Frankie was silent for a while as he seemed to consider his next words. "You sure you want things to go down like this?"

Davie nodded and stood firm, not breaking eye contact for a second.

Andrew sat and watched from the armchair, hardly able to breathe as he waited for an outcome of this familial confrontation – it seemed his life might hang in the balance. At least, if anything, he'd judged Davie correctly – the boy was nothing like his older brother.

"I let them go; I go down," said Frankie. "You want that?"

Davie sighed. "Course not. You're my blood."

"So what then? What would you have me do, Davie? You seem to be the one with all the answers so enlighten me."

He shrugged. "Just leave. They won't say anything."

Frankie laughed his head off. "You're shitting me? Course they will."

"Not if you threaten to send someone round to finish the job. Just like the kid in the bathtub – nothing gets said to the police and everything stays cool."

Everything will not be cool, thought Andrew as he looked across at his catatonic wife, bleeding from her butchered face beneath a bald head. This isn't going to end with you just walking away scot free. No way in hell.

Frankie took some time to think about things. Andrew did some thinking of his own. If Frankie did leave, then the first thing he would do was call the police. But if Frankie stayed, then he would certainly commit murder. If it was the latter outcome then Andrew wasn't going to go down without a fight. The agony of his tooth extraction had reawakened his senses to the point that they were on high alert. If he was going to save his family it would be now.

"I'm sorry," Frankie told his brother earnestly. "I can't leave things now. My business isn't done. Got to take this thing to the end."

I'll end it for you right now, you son of a bitch.

Andrew leapt from the armchair and barrelled into the back of Frankie as hard as he could. The body tackle sent Frankie forward with enough force that he flipped clear over the room's coffee table and landed awkwardly on his shoulder, crying out. Like angry bees, the twins were on Andrew in an instant.

Andrew lunged aside as Dom attempted to tackle him. The teen missed and went tumbling into the TV stand headfirst. Without thinking, Andrew swung his leg viciously and connected with the boy's ribs, enjoying the crunching sound it made. Michelle attacked next. The wicked little harlot screeched at him like a medieval war maiden and came at him with a pair of scissors. Andrew had no time to consider the ethics of hitting a girl so threw the hardest punch he could produce. Lips and teeth mushed beneath his colliding fist and Michelle flew backwards, already unconscious on her way down to the floor.

Next up was Jordan, and his attack was far more effective. He came at Andrew with his arms wide, embracing him in a crushing bear hug and ramming him into the nearest wall. Andrew lost his breath as his cracked ribs impacted against the hard plasterboard. Unable to free his arms, he did the only thing he could think of. He bit Jordan in the face as hard as he could, teeth slicing through the succulent flesh and causing a high-pitched, agonising scream. Jordan's struggling just made Andrew bite down harder, and he didn't release his grip until a fatty chunk of flesh fell away in his mouth. He spat the morsel onto the ruined carpet and pushed the shuddering teen away from him.

Andrew felt as though he was outside of his body now, controlling his rage-infected limbs from far away as they coursed with murderous intent. After being captured and subdued like an animal, he was finally free – and all he wanted now was to see the blood of his captors flow as freely as his own.

But before he had a chance to sow his vengeance and free his family, he found himself, once again, powerless. Frankie stood in front of the sofa, a knife to Bex's throat. She was still bound and gagged but Andrew could tell by his daughter's eyes that she was terrified.

"Just let her go, Frankie, and I'll let you walk out of here alive."

Frankie cackled. "You'll let me walk out of here alive. It's you that's a dead man."

Andrew shook his head. "Shoes on the other foot now. I'm going to rip you apart first opportunity I get. Best chance you've got is to run."

Frankie stared at Andrew as if he were insane. "You for real? I'd kill you before you even got close to me. I'm Frankie-fuckin-Walker."

Andrew shook his head. "You're just a sad little boy who probably got raped in prison. We should all feel sorry for you – but you made a huge mistake when you took it out on my family. You're a dead man."

Davie entered the conversation, standing between them both. Jordan was still screaming in pain and rushed into the kitchen to tend to the ripped-open wound on his face. His brother Dom lay on the floor, rubbing his shoulder gingerly. Michelle was still unconscious. Davie put a hand up to Andrew and Frankie, like a referee at an out-of-hand boxing match. "Let's just keep things calm, okay? If you stay where you are, Andrew, we'll all get out of your house right now."

"Like fuck we will," said Frankie, still holding Rebecca at knifepoint.

Davie turned to his brother. "This has gone tits-up, bro. We need to bounce."

Frankie stared at his younger brother and eventually let out a sigh. "You're right. This is an epic fuckin' fail, man."

Davie nodded. "Let's not make it any worse."

"Okay. Dom, get up off the floor and fetch your brother from the kitchen. Get Michelle up and carry her useless ass out of here." Frankie looked at Andrew, narrowed his eyes. "You come after me, gangster, and I'll put you down for good. Then someone will come and sort your family out for good measure. Same thing will happen if you go to the police. You get me?"

Andrew said nothing. He didn't need to involve himself in worthless banter with a degenerate like Frankie – he could see through it all now. The police would get a call the moment he left, and if anyone came after Andrew's family afterwards, they would be made to regret it. There was a beast inside of him that had been created and let out.

"Let my daughter go and leave."

It wasn't Andrew who spoke. It was Pen. She'd stood up from the sofa and was clutching the scissors in her hand. No one had seen her grab them, but in the ruckus that had erupted she would have had every chance to take them.

"Let her go," Pen repeated, pointing the scissors at Frankie's face. "Now."

Frankie sniggered. "Or else what, you bald bitch?"

"I'll kill you."

Andrew called out to his wife and tried to calm her down. The situation was nearly over and she didn't need to do this. "Honey, come over to me. Everything is going to be okay in just a minute."

But Pen wasn't listening. She had a haunted look like she was somewhere else entirely; somewhere where only she and Frankie existed, with Bex in the middle.

"Listen to your husband, sweetheart. You ain't going to be doing nuffin'. Come near me and I stick your whore daughter."

Pen let out a roar and rushed at Frankie with the scissors, her face contorted in a witch-like grimace of utter hatred and malevolence. Frankie spun to meet her head on, holding Bex in front of him as a shield. Their bodies collided and the scissors disappeared in the tussle.

Andrew's heart froze, along with every other muscle of his body. As he stood there in terror. The next several seconds passed like an eternity, until Frankie pushed Bex against her mother and stepped away, snarling. Andrew saw the blood immediately. Then he saw the scissors jutting out from his daughter's stomach as she fell to the floor in shock. Pen looked down at Bex and let out an inhuman wail, then she lunged at Frankie, aiming her sharp fingernails at his remorseless eyes.

Frankie struck out with the knife and Pen stumbled right into it. There was no sound as the blade entered the soft tissue of her throat and, for a moment, Andrew wasn't sure if the injury was as real as it looked. When blood spurted high enough to coat the ceiling, the reality of the situation became undeniably real.

"Stupid bitch," said Frankie, looking down at her. "Dom, Jordan, go get Michelle, right now. We're leaving."

Andrew dropped to his knees, oblivious to the escaping youths that had made his life a living hell before destroying it completely. The only thing that existed in his life right now was Penelope and Rebecca, and both of them were dying on the living room floor.

-19-

"Shit man. This is bad. Why the hell did you do that, Frankie?" Davie struggled to keep up with the others as they ran deeper into the estate, passing by rows of houses that became progressively smaller and unkempt as they left the better areas. Usually he would have been faster than the lot of them, but his throbbing concussion meant he could manage no more than a lolloping walk.

Frankie slowed down and allowed Davie to catch up. "Bitch had it coming," he said. "She came at me like a nutcase, you saw it."

"I saw you drive a knife into her neck when you could have just as easily punched her."

Frankie shrugged. "It's done now. No point stressing about it."

Davie reached out and grabbed his brother's jacket, dragging them both to a stop. "You're tripping, bro. The police will be after us all within the next two minutes. There're two woman bleeding to death because of you!"

Frankie huffed. "Because of us."

Davie shook his head, dismayed by the suggestion that he was to blame for any part of this. "What the hell did I do?"

"You distracted me enough that Andrew could take a shot at me. Everything went tits-up after that. If you'd just kept your gob shut then everything would have been okay. I was just about to let them go, little bro. Figured I'd them enough to get the message."

"Bullshit," said Davie, hoping there was zero truth to his brother's words. "You told everyone you were going to kill Andrew."

"Course I did," said Frankie. "I wanted him to shit himself. I weren't gunna do it, though. You think I'm a complete muppet or what?"

Davie shook his head. He was feeling dizzy again and couldn't wait to find his way to bed. Were his actions really the cause of what had happened? Davie wasn't sure he could live with himself if they were. He stared at Frankie and concentrated on his brother's reactions. "You were really just going to let them go?"

Frankie put a hand on his brother's shoulder and looked him dead in the eye. "I swear, man. They were at the point where they would never have said shit to no one. The pigs wouldn't have ever known. Now though..."

"What are we going to do?"

Frankie patted Davie on the back and got them both moving again. Up ahead, the twins and a groggy Michelle were waiting for them. "We're going to go see a mate of mine and lay low for a while at his gaff. We'll get our stories straight and decide what we're going to do then."

Davie nodded. "Okay. Who's this mate? Can we trust him?"

"Yeah," said Frankie. "It's him I've been dealing product for. Well, his old man, really, but he's in the nick for a stretch."

"Maybe, we should just go home instead. Get mum to tell the police we've been home all night."

"You really want to rely on that drunk bitch to keep a story straight?"

"I suppose not."

They caught up with the others at the end of the street just as they passed by a group of shops and a grotty old pub called The Trumpet.

"My mate lives a few blocks up," Frankie told them all. "It's pretty late so he should be in. Mind your manners though because this guy would kill you as soon as look at you. In fact he's the only geezer in the world that actually scares me. "

Everyone nodded their understanding. Then they got going again, heading through the paved jungle of the housing estate and disappearing into the night.

***

Frankie knocked the door and shushed everyone. The house they were standing at was bigger than most of the others on the street, with a long driveway and an overhanging porch that had a light that lit their approach.

"He going to be mad?" Davie asked, trying to fight away the feeling that things were somehow getting worse not better.

"Maybe," said Frankie, "but once I tell him the deal, he'll understand. Last thing he needs is his best dealer going away for a long stretch."

A light came on in the hallway. It shined through the frosted glass of the PVC door, and after a few seconds of clinking sounds, of deadbolts and chains being unlocked, the door opened up. Blinking out at them through sleep-fuzzed eyes was a shaven-headed youth about the same age as Frankie. The lad was well-muscled and wearing nothing but a pair of designer boxer-shorts.

"Fuck, Frankie, is that you?"

"Yeah, Damien, it's me. I need to lay low for a couple days. Some shit went down that's pretty heavy."

Damien glanced at a glinting watch on his wrist and narrowed his eyes beneath the glaring porch light. "Two-o-clock in the morning, man. You pick your goddamn times, you know that? I ought to whoop your ass for waking me."

"I know, man. If I wasn't desperate, I wouldn't be here."

Damien opened the door wider and let them all in. "You'll make this up to me, Frankie. We'll discuss it later."

They all entered and Damien closed and locked the door behind them. He ushered them through into the lounge where Davie peered around in awe. A plasma screen TV as big as any he'd seen hung from the far wall, while opposite was a huge wraparound sofa deep enough to bury ten bodies in. Everything was expensive, and the fact that it belonged to someone only a few years older than Davie made it even more unbelievable. He could see why Frankie had allowed himself to get dragged down the same path of dealing drugs if these were the rewards.

"Take a seat," Damien told everyone. "I'll get some beers and put the heating on. They say it's going to snow this year and it's already getting too cold for my liking. Frankie you come with me and we'll talk business."

Davie watched his brother leave and sat himself down on the extravagant sofa. The twins and Michelle did the same.

"What a fucking trip," said Dom. "Never seen nothing like what happened tonight."

"We're all screwed," Davie said glumly.

"Stop stressing, D," said Michelle. "Frankie will sort everything out."

Davie didn't want to talk to any of them. They understood what they'd all been party to, and they didn't care - monsters. Davie, on the other hand, couldn't help but recall the images of Rebecca hitting the floor with the scissors poking out of her guts. She hadn't hurt anyone and neither had her mother. Now they were both probably dead.

What was it about Andrew that had consumed all of Frankie's focus? The torture of that poor family had been like an obsession once he'd gotten into their house. Davie thought about Andrew now and considered the pain the man must be feeling after watching his family get destroyed like that. Maybe it was the worst pain imaginable. It certainly seemed like it at the time as Davie had watched the man bellow.

"You think Frankie will let us score some more?" Jordan asked the group.

"I hope so," his twin added. "I'm starting to come down big-style. My face is killing me. Can you believe that crazy fucker bit a chunk out of my cheek? It's still bleeding now and I feel well-sick."

"I just wanna sleep," said Michelle. "I'm knackered and my face is mashed-up. Think I lost a tooth."

"You ain't getting no sleep tonight, sweetheart," said Damien, re-entering the lounge. "You and me are going upstairs."

Michelle frowned at him. "The fuck you talking about? I'm Frankie's girl."

"Exactly," said Damien, "and Frankie owes me. Consider yourself rent for the bunch of you staying here tonight. You may be a bit of a bruised-up mess, but you'll do, I suppose."

"No fucking way. Frankie wouldn't let anyone else have me."

Frankie entered the room and Damien winked at him. "Is that right Frankie? Seems your girl is playing hard to get."

"Just get your ass upstairs," Frankie told Michelle, clicking his fingers at her. "I'll see you in the morning."

Michelle glanced around the room, looking rescue, but the twins just shrugged and Davie wasn't about to offer her any assistance either. Far as he was concerned, Michelle deserved everything she got. Maybe it was time for her to learn a lesson.

Michelle stood up, looking confused but unable to find an argument, so she turned to Damien. "You serious? You want me to go upstairs and fuck you?"

Damien laughed. "I'm going to be the one fucking you." He offered out his hand and Michelle took it reluctantly. Damien turned to Frankie and winked on his way out of the room. "I'll see you in the morning. Oh, and that other favour you needed from me...you'll find it in a box beneath the sofa. Have fun, kids."

"You too," said Frankie, although he didn't seem to mean it. His face twitched several times as he watched Michelle be led away.

Frankie collapsed down onto the sofa and kicked off his trainers, letting out a loud sigh. Davie waited for him to say something, but it appeared he was quite content to close his eyes and go right to sleep. Apparently murder and mayhem wasn't enough to keep Frankie awake.

Davie asked him a question, before he had a chance to drop off. "You okay with Damien banging Michelle?"

Frankie didn't move or even open his eyelids as he spoke. "I was the one that suggested it, bro. Easy way to settle a debt, innit?"

"She's your bird, though."

"Fuck Shell. She's happy as long as she's got coke in her nose and a cock up her ass. Who gives a damn?"

"Didn't look like she wanted to go," said Dom. "Look on her face was classic."

The sound of frantic fucking suddenly emanated from above them. The ceiling began to vibrate and the light fixtures swung back and forth. Two voices could be heard moaning in ecstasy – both Damien and Michelle's.

"She sounds alright to me," said Frankie. "Now, everyone get their head down for a few hours. I can't be doing with anymore thinking right now. We'll sort shit out in the morning. I'll make some calls and get a few ears to the ground – see what's happening."

Everyone seemed more than happy to oblige. It had been a long and frantic night for all of them and no one wanted to get shuteye more than Davie. Before he did, though, he had one last question for his big brother.

"What's in a box under the sofa, Frankie?"

Frankie's voice was dreamy, already half-asleep. "You'll find out in the morning, little bro." Then he was fast asleep and snoring. It was almost an hour before Davie managed to join him. The sound of Michelle getting fucked upstairs kept him awake.

-20-

The nurses made Andrew wait outside and he'd been forced to wait in an empty corridor while Pen and Bex were rushed into separate operating theatres. Nurses now rushed back and forth between the two rooms, glancing apprehensively at Andrew each time they passed him. Their expressions were always grim and pitying. A bad sign.

Andrew's own wounds– serious in their own right –needed looking at, too, but he refused anyone who tried to take him away. He was unwilling to move until he knew the fate of his family. If only he could take their place. If he died, Pen and Bex would still have each other, but if they died, then he would have nothing – his life would remain an empty husk forever, containing nothing more than memories of the things taken away from him.

Frankie would pay for this, one way or another.

"Mr Goodman?"

Andrew looked up to see a pair of familiar faces. He smiled at them as best he could, but it felt like an obscene gesture considering what had happened. "Officers, what are you doing here?"

"Are you okay?" asked Dalton. "We've had reports of multiple stabbings. A man, his daughter, and wife."

"We were really hoping it wasn't you," said Wardsley, shaking his head solemnly, "but we had a bad feeling."

Andrew huffed with exasperation but it came out more like a hiss. "Looks like your feeling was right."

The two officers took a seat on the bench beside him and leant forward so that they could both see him and each other. For the first time since Andrew had seen them, neither was taking notes. They weren't there to take his statement; at least not right now.

"Was this all down to Frankie?" Dalton asked.

Andrew ran a hand across his forehead and rubbed at his tired eyes that had begun to itch. It must have been close to dawn by now. "Frankie and his mates did this, yes."

"You have names for any of them?"

"I got their first names but no surnames. One of the kids was Frankie's younger brother, though. I know because I admitted the lad here at the hospital last night after I hit him with my car."

Wardsley was wide-eyed. "You ran him over?"

"Not on purpose. It was an accident. A coincidence, if you can believe that. I rushed the boy here straight away and gave him a lift home afterwards. Frankie found out about it."

"He probably thought you did it intentionally," Dalton suggested.

Andrew nodded. "Didn't matter that his little brother tried telling him the truth. Frankie wanted his fun. Now my girls are in surgery, maybe dying...maybe already dead."

Wardsley growled. "We'll get him for this, Mr Goodman, I promise you."

"You think so? I mean, honestly, do you think you'll put him away and keep him there? What if he has twenty people giving him an alibi?"

The look on the officer's faces told Andrew all he needed to know. "Don't worry about it," he told them with a wave of his hand. "I know it's not your fault."

Wardsley sighed. "We will do all that we can. He won't get away with this."

"But what made him this way?" Andrew asked them, unable to fathom the answer. "Lots of kids grow up with a bad upbringing, but it's more than that with Frankie. He's rotten to the core. There's nothing there where his heart should be."

Dalton shook her head. "I wish there were an answer that made some sense, but there's not. We made some calls to the borstal that he was kept at. One of the guards who knew him told us that during his first year he was bullied severely by the other inmates – maybe that has something to do with it. He certainly changed during those following years."

"What do you mean?"

Wardsley took over from his partner. "This guard told us that by the time he left, Frankie was running the show. Top dog. A complete turnaround. He also told us... I shouldn't really say."

"What?" demanded Andrew. "Tell me."

"Well," Wardsley continued, "all of the other youth offenders who had bullied Frankie in his first year were badly injured – one by one throughout the course of a few months. Every one of them was... impaled."

"Impaled?"

Wardsley nodded. "Violated by a blunt object – typically pool cues from the Rec Room. None of them would talk about what happened afterwards. One boy died of a perforated rectum."

Andrew grimaced. "Jesus."

"We think that perhaps these other residents of the offender's home abused Frankie during his first year and he took a fitting revenge on them. To say it left him with some severe emotional problems is an understatement to say the least."

"That's horrible," said Andrew, "but it doesn't make what he's done okay. He's still a monster, whatever he's been through."

"I agree," said Wardsley. "He'll never change now."

"But chances are he'll be back on the streets to hurt other people?"

"We'll get him," said Dalton. "We'll charge him with attempted murder and do everything we can for you and your family. You need to trust us."

Andrew sighed. "But even if he goes away, it won't be forever, right?"

"I can't say," Dalton admitted.

Andrew had heard enough. "I don't need to hear it."

Wardsley and Dalton both put their hands up to calm him. "I know, Andrew. We wanted to check on you, to see if you need anything?"

Andrew looked at the officers, examined the concern on their faces and looked for gaps. It seemed genuine and he was left with little doubt that these two police officers were just people like anybody else. They emphathised with Andrew's pain and despised the fact that demons like Frankie could walk the earth almost unobstructed. Their offer of assistance was real, but right now Andrew had no clues what to ask for – or if he even needed anything from them at all.

Before he had a chance to reply, a fully-scrubbed surgeon stepped out of one of the operating theatres and approached him with caution. "Mr Goodman?"

Andrew stood up, his knees shaking uncontrollably. "Yes, that's me."

The surgeon nodded and smiled. "Your daughter has been stabilised for now. There is some damage to the digestive tract that could possibly cause complications later or some lasting damage, but we've managed to stem any internal bleeding and she's no longer in critical condition."

Andrew didn't absorb a single word. None of what the doctor said had informed him with absolute certainty what he really needed to know. "Is she going to make it?"

The surgeon nodded. "Barring anything unexpected your daughter should make a full recovery. As I said, the damage to her large intestine could cause some issues, but nothing that can't be managed. You'll be able to see her in a few hours when we move her somewhere more comfortable."

Andrew let out a sigh of relief that seemed to go on forever. He heard similar sounds from the police officers behind him. "What about my wife?" he asked the surgeon, moving on to his next concern now that the previous one was over.

The surgeon shook his head and seemed apologetic. Andrew fought away the overwhelming urge to vomit as the man spoke the words he didn't want to hear. "I'm afraid Dr Killarney is the attending for your wife, so I can't give you much information. From my cursory examination of her wounds, however, I would not be optimistic. I'm sorry, Mr Goodman, but I doubt she'll pull through."

Andrew felt all the blood in his body drop to his feet and he collapsed backwards. Officer Wardsley caught him, directing his fall towards the bench and setting him down on it.

Andrew looked the man dead in the eyes and said, "I need a favour."

-21-

Sunshine crept into the room and bathed Davie's face. His eyelids fluttered as his pupils reacted to the light and it took him a few minutes to open them fully. Once a little more awake he looked around himself to get his bearings. The living room was foreign and bizarre but, after a few moments, he recalled the memories of last night. This was Damien's place; the current location of his ongoing nightmare.

No one else inhabited the room and Davie had the entire sofa to himself. He was alone in someone else's house and suddenly felt very vulnerable.

"Everyone has gone back to their own gaffs," said Frankie from behind him, standing in the doorway.

"Didn't you want us all to stick together?"

Frankie walked into the room and sat on the futon opposite the sofa. "At first, yeah, but Damien told me that if the police come and find us in a group matching the exact description that a victim gave it would corroborate their evidence. I gave everyone their stories and sent them on their way. They know what to say, so don't worry."

"I'm not worried," said Davie. "I don't know what I feel. Last night was fucked up, bro."

Frankie nodded in agreement, seeming to reminisce about the events unfavourably. "Should never have gone down that way, man. Way too messy, leaving things like that. Jordan's face was messed up this morning – think it's infected or something. My fault. Should have dealt with things better... more neatly."

"What do you mean?" asked Davie. "You should have killed them?"

Frankie shrugged. "Maybe. Too late now. We just need to be ready."

"Ready how?"

Frankie smiled and tilted his body forward, sliding off the futon and onto his knees. He slipped an arm beneath the sofa and retrieved a flat wooden box, then placed it carefully onto his lap.

Davie frowned. "What's in it?"

"Our insurance policy." Frankie unfastened the pair of brass clips on either end of the box and popped the lid.

Davie couldn't believe what was inside. "Guns? Are you crazy?"

"Chill the fuck out. They're just in case that nutcase comes after us. I ain't going to play with this guy no more."

"Nutcase?" Davie was dumbfounded. "We held him hostage and stabbed his family. I think he has good reason to be a little nutty."

"Whatever," said Frankie dismissively. "If he comes at me he's going to taste lead...or whatever the stuff is they make bullets out of nowadays. Quit your bitching and take this."

Frankie thrust one of the revolvers at Davie who immediately shoved it right back. "I will not. I don't want a gun."

Frankie pushed harder until he had no choice but to take ownership of the weapon. "Just keep it in your waistband," he asked. "You don't have to go looking for trouble, but I want to know you're safe if that prick comes after you."

"Andrew."

"What?"

"His name is Andrew."

Frankie shook his head in confusion. "Does it look like I give a monkey's nuts?"

"No," said Davie. "No it doesn't. Fine, I'll take the gun, but only for protection. What about the twins? Did you give them guns?"

"Fuck them. They can fend for themselves. Only person I care about is you."

"Hope I'm not breaking up a Hallmark moment." Damien entered the room and stood in front of them. Everything he was wearing was emblazoned with a logo of some kind.

Frankie looked up at him from the sofa. “Nah, man, everything’s cool. Was just getting my little bro strapped.”

Damien nodded. “What’s your next move?”

“Don’t know. Either the police will turn up at my door or this guy that has a beef with me will. I’ll be ready for whatever happens, though, thanks to you.” He waved the gun as though it were a toy and not a deadly weapon.

“You get caught with that you leave my name out of it, you hear me? They belong to my old man and he’d go ape if he knew I was lending ‘em out. Can’t have you dead, though, can I? Need you out on the street. What you do to this dude anyway? You can’t have just fucked up his car and house.”

“We stabbed his wife and daughter,” Davie blurted out. The sudden confession made him feel better.

Damien’s eyes widened and his eyebrows lowered into a scowl. “The fuck? The hell you do that for? You don’t fuck with a man’s family – with women.”

Frankie waved a hand dismissively. “Shit went down. That’s all there is to it. You’re one to talk, anyway, man. You fuck people up all the time.”

“Business,” said Damien. “I don’t fuck up innocent families. Did this guy even do anything to you?”

“No,” said Davie. “He never done nothing to nobody.”

Frankie turned to Davie and growled. “Will you shut the hell up!”

“Sounds like your little bro has a conscience,” said Damien. “Good for him. You both need get the fuck out of my house now.”

Frankie stood up. “What? Why you being like this?”

“Cus you’re a fucking mug, an amateur. Now piss off – and leave the pieces behind. I ain’t gunna risk you shooting up some more innocent families.”

Frankie didn’t hand the gun over; he pulled the revolver on Damien and cocked the hammer. Davie wondered how his brother even knew how to do that.

Damien’s face was unflinching, unlike Frankie’s which was twitching madly.

“I hope this dude fucks you up,” Damien said. “Makes you a little bitch again like you used to be when I met you in the nick.”

Frankie stepped forward and shoved the barrel against Damien’s forehead. His whole arm was shaking but Damien was still unflinching. “Not another word, Damien, or I’ll end you right now.”

Davie stood up and moved beside his brother, trying to attract the attention of his demented stare. “What’s he talking about, Frankie? What happened in the nick?”

Damien directed his gaze to Davie casually, unbothered by the gun against his forehead. "Your big bro never tell you?

"Tell me what?"

"When I went down for a little stretch – for dealing and shit – they sent me to the same nick as Frankie."

Frankie thrust the revolver forward, jarring Damien's head back. "Not another word. I'm warning you."

Damien continued anyway. "Your big tough bro here was the prison bitch for a whole year. Fell in bad with the top dogs when he arrived – mouthing off and acting like a gangster before he even knew the score. Spent the next year getting it up the shitter by half the guys on G Wing."

"Bullshit," said Davie. "You're talking bollocks."

Damien winked at Davie. "God's honest truth, little man. When I arrived, my dad's rep was enough for me to be one of the top dogs straight away. I put a stop to all that stuff – shit stabbing's really not my thing. Your brother was so grateful that he offered to do anything for me in return. Just so happened that I needed some help shifting gear when I got out. The rest is history."

"Is this all true?" Davie asked Frankie, who seemed like he was going to go off like a firework, veins bulging through the hot redness of his skin.

Frankie sniffed back a nose full of snot and recovered himself. "Guy's full of it. He did me a few solids during our time together, that much is true. In fact the only reason he ain't dead right now is because I owe him."

"Owe me big time," Damien added. "Big time."

Frankie nodded. "Lucky for you, I honour my debts – but consider us even."

Damien smiled from behind the gun barrel. "Fair enough. Say goodbye to your supply though. You find out who your friends are when you're not holding all the time. Tell Dom and Jordan to come see me in The Trumpet. Maybe they can take your old job."

"Whatever," said Frankie. "Come on Davie. Let's get the fuck out of here."

Still pointing the revolver at Damien's face, Frankie backed out of the room. Davie followed after him, shell shocked by what he'd just heard. There was every chance that Damien was just making shit up to mess with Frankie. But if it were true...

Then Davies big brother was messed up for a reason.

"Hey, Davie," said Damien as they went to leave. "Don't end up like your brother, yeah?"

Davie said nothing, just left the room with Frankie. Together they navigated the long hallway towards the front door and let themselves out. The cold air of the afternoon hit Davie in the face like a punch, making his teeth ache.

"Getting cold," he said, rubbing at his shoulders.

Frankie shrugged. "Other things to worry about right now."

"No shit," Davie agreed. Yet somehow he couldn't help but think about the weather. He had a feeling that there was going to be a storm of epic proportions.

And the first drops of rain had just fallen.

-22-

Officer Wardsley and Officer Dalton had refused Andrew's request to locate Frankie for him – they didn't want him taking the law into his own hands – so now he was sitting at his wife's bedside wondering what to do. It was approaching 5pm, the morning having come and gone in a whirlwind of grief and emotion. Bex was yet to wake up but the Doctors had assured him she would do do soon – that her body was just taking the opportunity to rest. Pen's condition was less optimistic.

Her surgery had ended a couple hours ago and she was now lying deathly still. Stitches and gauze covered her throat while a drip entered the artery of her right arm, supplying her body with whatever it was that the Doctors thought it needed.

"I'll make this right," Andrew whispered to his dying wife. "I'll make them pay for what they've done – for what they've done to you and Rebecca."

Pen said nothing.

He sat for a while and listened to the silence, wishing beyond all hope that the woman he loved would sit up and say something. It wasn't going to happen, though – might not ever happen.

Tears fell from his eyes and stained the thin white cotton sheets that covered his wife's injured body. "I failed you, Pen. It's my job to keep you safe. How can I ever forgive myself? If you die, how will I go on? I've loved you since the day we met. Life wouldn't make sense without you. Please don't go." He leant forward and laid his head against her stomach. He could hear her heart pumping – slow and steady – the pause between each beat a balancing act between life and death. "Please don't leave me, Pen. Our daughter needs you."

"Sorry to interrupt," said a young blonde nurse, entering the room, "but your daughter has just woken up."

Andrew's stomach churned and he had to swallow back a mouthful of stomach acid.

What the hell did he say to her? A kid shouldn't have to deal with something like this.

Andrew got up, kissed his wife's forehead, then followed the nurse out of the room. Both Penelope and Rebecca had been moved once their surgery concluded and were now in separate parts of the building. Pen was in ICU under constant watch, while Bex was in the convalescence ward. They were on separate floors and it took Andrew five minutes of marching through a maze of corridors to reach his daughter's room.

Although obviously weak, Bex smiled at him as soon as he entered the room. his heart ached at the sight of her. Dark-brown hair matted her forehead and her usually rosy complexion had turned ashen. She looked like a zombie from one of the films she loved to watch.

"Hey," Andrew said as he placed himself down on a cheap plastic chair beside the bed. "How are you feeling, sweetheart?"

"Like I got stabbed with a pair of scissors."

Andrew grinned, happy that his daughter's sense of humour had not been damaged despite everything. "Arts and crafts never were your strong point, Bex."

"How's mum?"

He had hoped the question would wait, that his daughter would not remember events so much as to realise that she was not the only one who'd been injured. Telling Bex that her mother might be dying would not be good for her own recovery.

But he couldn't lie to her, not his own daughter.

"She's bad, sweetheart. The doctors have told us to wait and see, but right now she's not responding. Her surgery went okay, though, which is a good sign. We have to hold on to the positives."

Bex looked her father in the eyes and wore an expression that seemed to hold more sadness than should have been possible for such a young girl. "Why did they do this to us, Dad?"

Andrew shook his head and looked down at the floor. "I don't know. Really, I don't."

"They would have killed us all if you hadn't done something."

Andrew sighed. "I got you both stabbed!"

"It would have been worse if you'd done nothing."

"I might not have gotten the chance if Davie hadn't tried to put a stop to things first."

Bex looked concern. "You think he'll be okay? What if the others blame him?"

Andrew shrugged his shoulders and winced at the pain that shot through his ribs. "To be honest the only people I'm concerned about are you and your mother. Davie still sat and watched Frankie tortured us. He did what was right at the end, but it wasn't enough."

"Don't be angry, Dad."

Andrew looked at his daughter. "Don't be angry. Are you joking?"

She shook her head wearily. "If you're angry then you're just letting them get away with even more. Of course I want them all arrested and sent to prison...for-like-ever...but I won't let them inside my head. They don't deserve to change who we are, Dad. You're not an angry person, so don't let them make you one."

Andrew couldn't believe his daughter was so willing to move on. Would she feel the same way if the doctors came in and told her that her mother was dead? Would she let anger into her heart then? Andrew understood what his daughter was saying, but it was too late to put aside his emotions – anger had already infested his soul and taken root. There was no going back to the man he was before. That mad was dead.

He needed to change the subject, for dwelling on the subject was already making his heart grow heavy with rage. "Should I go home and get you some things, sweetheart? What would you like?"

Bex smiled at him, but seemed trapped in a constant state of drowsiness – as if she could not escape the fringes of sleep. "That would be nice," she muttered. "Can you pick me up some magazines from the shop? Then I just want my iPod and my... phone."

Andrew thought about his own phone. He had not called work in days and would probably not have a job to return to anymore. He put such worries aside, for now they seemed utterly unimportant. He gave Bex a warm smile to match the one she had given him. "I'll go home now and get them for you. I won't be long, but you try and get some rest in the meantime."

Bex nodded and already seemed to be falling into a deep sleep, so he exited the room quietly and went out into the corridor that was bustling with staff and patients. An old man ambled past, trundling a dripstand behind him, and said, hello. Andrew said it back to him and was surprised that pleasantries were still within his capabilities.

Andrew went up to the nurse's station and asked a question. "Is there somewhere I can find a taxi?"

The nurse nodded. "There's a small taxi rank on the eastside of the car park. Can't miss it."

Andrew hadn't seen it when he'd entered the hospital, but then he had not been paying attention to such things. His plan was to catch a taxi home, get Bex's things, then immediately return via taxi as well – he wasn't up to driving with his nerves the way they were.

The corridor on his left had an EXIT sign so he took it. It led through to a waiting room and then straight out into the car park. Before he left, he noticed something and stopped. His heart rose up into his throat, filling his mouth with the taste of copper.

Sat in a nearby waiting room, looking extremely sorry for himself, was one of the twins – Jordan, if Andrew wasn't mistaken. The bite wound on the boy's perspiration-soaked face was glistening with pus and blood. Infection had set in and the boy looked in a great deal of discomfort. Andrew was glad.

But it wasn't enough. Jordan would recover and put the whole thing behind him like it had all been one big giggle.

Andrew moved to the rear of the room behind Jordan, so that the youth would not see him. Of the options available, none seemed clear. He could call Wardsley and Dalton, but had little faith that they could do much other than hold the boy for a day or two. The twin's parents would probably turn up and have him released. The other option was to attack the son of a bitch right now – to wring the little bastard's neck – but that would result only in his own arrest. Andrew took a seat and decided to wait and think.

***

Twenty minutes later a nurse called out a name: Jordan Ebanks. Andrew watched the boy get up and then slowly followed after him, making sure to stay several steps behind. The nurse took Jordan into a consultation area that contained two rows of adjustable gurneys inside curtained surroundings. Jordan hopped up on one of the beds, but then the nurse pulled the curtain closed and Andrew lost sight of him.

He crept forward and tried to look inconspicuous by nodding hello to anyone who noticed him. Putting his head down, he hurried over to Jordan's cubicle and stopped just outside of it. He listened to the conversation coming from inside.

"How did it happen?" asked the female voice that belonged to the nurse. "Looks like a bite mark."

"Got jumped by some nutter, innit; think he was a crackhead or something. Must have thought he was a zombie or summin cus he took a chunk outta me."

Lying little shit, Andrew thought. Why don't you tell her what really happened?

"Well," said the nurse, "if that is what happened then you should inform the police."

Jordan sucked at his teeth. "Don't deal with the pigs, sweetheart. I deal with my biz'nis direct, if you get me?"

The nurse ignored the boy's bravado and carried on with her job diligently. Andrew assumed she had heard such nonsense before and paid it little mind. "I'll get this bandaged for you," she said, "but then you'll need a course of general antibiotics. If it gets any worse you'll need to come back."

"Sound," said Jordan. "I'll make sure I ask for you, sweetheart."

"If you wish," replied the nurse, unable to sound any less-interested. "I'm just going to get a doctor for your prescription, then I'll come get you dressed up."

"I like getting undressed better," Jordan quipped, but the nurse had already exited the cubicle.

Now that the boy was alone, Andrew found himself frozen. He hadn't thought about what he would do next, and without a game plan, he allowed his instincts to take over. He slipped inside the curtain and faced Jordan.

The boy's bloodshot eyes went wide. "Jesus Christ! The fuck you doing here?"

"You put my entire family in hospital. Where the hell did you think I'd be, you moron?"

"Man, you must be outta your mind, frontin' on me!"

Andrew took a step closer, a snarl on his lips. "You almost kill my family, yet you can flirt with the fucking nurse like nothings happened. You think I'm the one who's out of my mind? You're a monster."

"Hey, that shit was Frankie's deal. I was just along for the ride, blud, you gte me?"

"Well you won't have a problem telling the police what happened then?"

Jordan's sickly face turned sour. "I ain't saying shit to no one – especially the pigs. Frankie's my boy and I don't know what you're talking about anyway. I ain't seen him in weeks. If someone took it to your family then they must've had it coming."

Before Andrew had any chance to realise what he was doing, he'd thrown a punch at Jordan hard enough to knock the boy right off the bed.

"Motherfucker!" Jordan sprang back up to his feet immediately, lashing out at Andrew, not with his fists, but with a blade that he had suddenly produced from somewhere. "You lost your mind, whitey?"

Andrew didn't retreat. He rushed foreard to meet the boy and managed to get both hands around his knife-arm. A struggle ensued that sent the pair of them stumbling against the gurney. Andrew had the advantage of leverage, and managed to get above Jordan and forced him down against the bed. The knife pointed straight at Andrew's face but it got no closer. In fact, it began to move away. The tip of the blade twisted and shook, gradually pointing itself in the opposite direction. Towards Jordan.

Jordan's strength began to falter and the knife moved faster – perhaps it was the infection making him weak. Andrew realised that weapon was now under his control.

But what exactly did he want to happen? What the hell was he doing?

Despite his weakening struggles, Jordan still found the gall to spit in Andrew's face. "Fuckin' white-boy. You and your family are dead."

Andrew pushed down on the knife, applying all of his remaining strength and weight until the tip entered Jordan just below his bottom rib. All of the aggression disappeared and was replaced by the whimpering cries of a child. "P-please man... please don't. Don't!"

But this was no child in front of him. It was a monster.

Andrew pushed the knife in further and twisted it.

He watched the life drain from the Jordan's eyes.

He twisted the knife again. The last glimmers of life disappeared from the boy's eyes and his body slumped against the gurney.

Andrew peered down at the blood on his hands and could barely acknowledge what he'd just done. To murder a man was something impossible to him, yet he had just done it. Even more disturbing was that he didn't care about it one bit. In fact, he felt good about it. Not happy exactly, but at least satisfied.

Andrew felt the hairs prick up on the back of his neck. There was a presence behind him. He spun around to find the nurse standing behind him in shock, her mouth hanging wide open while her eyes fixated on the dead youth laying on her gurney.

"I'm sorry," Andrew told the woman, "he deserved it."

Then he ran.

-23-

Andrew managed to sprint right through the hospital and out into the car park without anyone stopping him. Other than a few funny looks, no one even seemed to notice him. Now that he was outside, he decided to slow down and disappear casually into the night.

Just as the male nurse had informed him, there was a small taxi rank on one side of the car park. It consisted of only two cars but he wasted no time in heading there. He realised that he was covered in blood, but most of it was on his hands, and only a small amount spattered his shirt. He wondered how he would explain it to the taxi driver, but wouldn't they be used to such things, picking up passengers from a hospital?

He reached the taxi and pulled open the rear door. The car was a featureless, silver saloon and the driver was a young Asian man who nodded at him as he entered the vehicle.

"Where to, my friend?"

Andrew gave his address and the driver set off, pulling out onto the main road speedily as if he had done so a thousand times before. It had gotten dark outside and the weather had started to worsen too. The rain increased gradually as if it had been waiting for night to fall before it could get started on its relentless tirade.

"Bad winter this year, my friend," said the driver, peering into the rear-view mirror to look at Andrew.

Andrew didn't want to make eye-contact so he looked down at his hands. His fingers were stiffening under a thick cake of Jordan's blood. "Yeah," he replied after a few seconds, deciding that making conversation would be less suspicious. "A lot of snow coming apparently. Hope there're no accidents on the road like last year. That was a bad one."

The driver nodded. "That poor man and his family? Drunk driver killed his wife and child?"

I know how he feels, thought Andrew, but then chastised himself for it. Bex was going to be okay and he would not know the loss of a child. He thanked God for that.

"The guy doesn't live that far from me actually," Andrew added. "He drinks in The Trumpet, I think."

"Rough in there," said the driver. "I've picked up some very nasty people."

"Wouldn't know," said Andrew. "Never been in there myself. Not much of a drinker."

"Best way, my friend. Alcohol never did anyone any good." The driver changed the subject. "So everything okay at the hospital? You look very tired. Hope it's not bad news."

"Just my grandfather," Andrew lied, shocked at the ease in which it came. "Cancer."

The driver glanced back over his shoulder and gave the obligatory sad face. "That's not good, my friend. I am sorry for you."

"It's fine. He's very old and he had a good life."

What was he saying? His grandfather had died twenty years ago.

There was silence in the car for the rest of the journey and perhaps the driver had sensed Andrew's discomfort in the way the conversation was going. Reading people was something taxi drivers probably got pretty good at.

"Where abouts, my friend?"

Andrew looked out the window to see that they had entered his street. It wasn't the wholesome grouping of quaint properties that it had been when he'd purchased the house several years ago. Things looked different now; a seedy underbelly exposed forever. There was an atmosphere of menace hanging over the street. Perhaps Andrew was the only one to sense it, but it was there now. An echo of violence.

"Just drop me here," he told the taxi driver. "Next to the red Mercedes."

The taxi driver pulled up next to Andrew's car and thankfully didn't seem to notice the graffiti all over it. He requested fifteen-pounds for the fare, which was extortionate for the small distance travelled, but Andrew didn't complain at the amount and paid twenty. Making another enemy was something he couldn't cope with right now – regardless of how inconsequential.

He thanked the driver and stepped out into the cold air and drizzle. The view of the street was a ghostly haze as the streetlights reflected off the falling rain. For some reason the taxi driver felt the need to say goodbye by beeping his horn and the sudden sharp honk made Andrew jump. His body still coursed with so much adrenaline that each droplet of rain hitting his tingling skin was like a pinprick.

He reached down into his jean pocket and pulled out his house keys, before heading down the path to his house and inserting them in the lock. Even from outside, the bloodstains were visible across the porch floor, leading all the way down the hallway beyond.

Upon entering his house, Andrew locked the porch behind him. Not something he would have worried about once, but the possibility of intruders had become a reality for him now. It wasn't just something that happened to other people anymore.

Andrew stepped through into the living room and was shocked by the chaos that met him. Despite being witness to how the room got into such a state, he still couldn't believe the amount of gore that matted everything – from the carpet to several small spots on the ceiling. The smell of mashed up fish and chips had been replaced by the far more noxious odour of metallic, tangy blood.

His family's blood.

Andrew collapsed onto the sofa, avoiding the armchair that had held him captive for almost an entire night, and began to put his thoughts in order. There was no way out of the mess he was in now. He had murdered a teenager in cold blood and had been witnessed doing so. At the time, the nurse had been transfixed by the sight of Jordan's mutilated body, but Andrew had no doubts that she would have seen his face.

Not to mention the amount of CCTV that a hospital is likely to have.

There was no getting out of the fact that very soon Andrew would be arrested and charged with murder. It likely wouldn't matter to the police his reasons why, but the only vindication he could hold onto was that Jordan was jointly responsible for the torture of his wife and child.

Jointly responsible...

What was going to happen to the others? Would they get away scot-free?

Andrew could take the punishment for what he'd done. What he couldn't take was if his actions somehow helped exonerate Frankie and the others. They would be free to blame the whole thing on Jordan now.

He done the whole thing, yer Honour. I had nothing to do with it.

And that was if they ever even went to court. They would provide alibis for one another and deny everything. That was exactly what Jordan had done right before Andrew gutted him like the cowardly fish that he was. He had been denying everything.

How good it would feel to do the same to Frankie.

Andrew passed over the thought, but then backed up and reconsidered it.

What was to stop him? He was going down for murder anyway. Pen might die and this could be the only chance to punish those responsible.

Somehow Andrew had found himself considering murder again. What shocked him most was that he'd already made his mind up. Looking around his smashed-up living room, covered in the blood of the people he loved, he was absolutely adamant that Frankie and his friends needed to die.

And they needed to die tonight.

Andrew leapt up from the sofa, the pain of his wounds forgotten as focus and determination crept in. He headed to the kitchen and straight for the drawer beneath the microwave. He took out the longest blade he could find – a 9-inch carving knife – and wrapped it up in a tea towel. He stuffed the whole thing down the waistband of his trousers, at the side so the blade wouldn't dig into him. Then he stood for a few moments, wondering if he should take anything else with him, but there was nothing more lethal inside the house than the knife he now possessed. He didn't need anything else. Just something he could kill Frankie with.

It was time to go.

He let out a long breath and enjoyed the calm for a moment, then stepped back through into the living room and took one final look at the mess of his home to reconfirm his intentions. There was still no doubt in his mind.

Into the hallway and through to the porch, Andrew unlocked the front door. The rain was falling harder now, hitting against the glass windows with the same ferocity of the blood pumping through his veins. He stepped out into the downpour and felt instantly refreshed as it washed away the drying blood from his skin. He ran his hands through his hair and slicked it back, squeezing away the excess moisture.

"Mr Goodman. Stay right where you are."

Andrew looked through the darkness and spotted two figures at the end of his path.

Officer Wardsley and Officer Dalton were there to arrest him.

***

"I don't have time for this," Andrew told the officers. "I need to go."

"Not going to happen," said Wardsley. "We need to ask you a few questions up at the station."

"I did it, alright? I murdered Jordan. You want to know why?"

The officers closed the gap between them and Andrew and now stood staring at him as though he were a wild animal.

"We know why," Dalton said, not unsympathetically.

"I murdered Jordan because he was one of the bastards who shaved my wife's head, snorted coke off her naked body, and then stabbed her and my daughter. I couldn't give him the chance to finish what he'd started. I couldn't let him walk around free to do it again."

Dalton stepped slightly ahead of her partner and looked at Andrew pityingly. "You should have left it to us, Andrew. They'll pay for what they've done, I promise. But now you're in a lot of trouble too. There's better ways to deal with people like Frankie and his friends. "

"Bullshit," Andrew spat. "You don't really believe that. They're all going to cover for each other and nothing will stick. Jordan was already pleading ignorant when I cornered him."

"Cornered him and murdered him," said Wardsley stepping up beside his partner. "You're no better than they are now."

Andrew examined both officers. If they were doing their jobs correctly, he would've already been in handcuffs by now, in their squad car and on his way to the station, but they were letting him talk.

"Do either of you have children?" he asked the both of them.

Both of them shook their heads.

"Then what do you know?"

"Nothing," Dalton admitted, "but you don't have the right to murder someone in a hospital right in front of frightened members of the public. That's not the right way."

Andrew laughed. "You sound like you disagree with my methods more than my actions."

The suggestion was met with silence. Andrew looked at Dalton and tried to read what she was thinking, but couldn't.

"You're going to go to prison, Mr Goodman," said Wardsley. "How does that help Rebecca?"

"It doesn't help her," he admitted. "But maybe by killing Jordan I've helped other people's daughters. He was just a teenager; plenty of years ahead of him for terrorising more innocent people."

"Maybe, you're right," said Wardsley, "but we still have to take you in."

Andrew nodded. "And I'll let you. Just let me finish what I started first."

Obviously the request shocked them both, because they looked at him like he was mad.

"I'm already going to prison," Andrew said. "Let me do some good before that happens. Let me make the world a safer place for other families, so that they don't end up like mine. Frankie is a cancer and I want to go and cut him out of the world."

"You're insane to even ask such a thing," said Wardsley. "It's ridiculous and I would suggest you don't say anything else. We are officers of the law."

Dalton stepped aside, leaving the pathway open and clear. She motioned with an arm that Andrew was free to walk by her. "You do what you have to do," she said, "but soon as you're finished you hand yourself in and confess everything."

Andrew nodded vigorously. "You have my word. Thank you."

"What the fuck are you doing, Laura?" said Wardsley, his eyes blinking in the rain. "You'll end up doing a stretch with him. Have you lost your mind?"

"I'm just letting him do what I would want to do in his situation, Jack. It's time these kids got a lesson taught to them. I'm sick of it, aren't you? These kids hang around in animal packs and put fear into everyone. It might be completely crazy, but I wouldn't mind tomorrow's newspapers telling a story about how one of the victims fought back."

Wardsley shook his head, exasperated. "If anyone finds out about this..."

"No one will," said Dalton, "and admit it – you want to see Frankie punished as well. Not just him but every arrogant little yob like him. We've been in the force almost ten years each, Jack, and in that time how many scumbags have we seen walk free, laughing all the way? Even when they go down, they don't care. They go about their business the moment they get back out. Wouldn't you like them to know that sometimes the victims can bite back?"

Wardsley thought about things for a moment and then seemed to relax his shoulders. It was clear he was struggling with something internally, but it was also clear that he trusted his partner. He stepped aside from the path and nodded at Andrew. “I don’t know how you’re going to find Frankie, but he’s been known to hang around with a local drug dealer named Damien Banks. 14 Middleton Mews. No collateral damage. Understand? Jesus, I can’t believe I’m doing this.”

Dalton slipped her hand into Wardsley’s and made it obvious the two were more than mere colleagues. For some reason, Andrew realised, Dalton empathised with him, and that had bought him a little time.

Andrew hurried past, sprinting down the path.

“Penelope’s dead,” Dalton shouted before he disappeared. “She died twenty minutes ago. I’m sorry.”

Andrew stopped, said nothing, didn’t turn around or even move. Instead he glared forward into the rain-soaked darkness with nothing but murder on his mind. “I’ll see you both in the morning,” he said to the officers, then disappeared into the night.

-24-

Davie waited anxiously for Frankie to get off the phone. His brother was clutching the mobile so tightly to his face that it threatened to break. Davie didn't know who was on the other end, or even what was being said, but he could tell one thing for certain: it was bad news.

"No fuckin' way," Frankie screamed into the phone. "How the hell did it happen?"

After several more minutes of shouting and cursing, Frankie ended the call and put the phone back in his jean pocket. He then proceeded to stand there saying nothing, staring at an invisible spot in the sky directly above his head.

"What is it?" Davie asked. "What's happened?"

Frankie lowered his gaze slowly until it focused on his brother. "Jordan's dead."

Davie could not have cared less about the twins, but the shock of hearing something so unexpected hit him in his stomach like a punch. There was no way Jordan could be dead.

I saw him last night.

Frankie elaborated. "That fucker bowled up to him at the hospital and gutted him."

Davie suddenly felt a fire in his tummy, which radiated throughout his entire body. He couldn't believe what he was hearing. "You mean Andrew did this?"

Frankie nodded angrily. "Dom heard a nurse give a description to the police. It was definitely him. Fucker's dead meat."

Davie still couldn't believe it. The thought of Andrew committing murder was insane. "What was Jordan doing at the hospital? He should have known Andrew would be there with his family."

"He was getting his face checked out. Dom said his bro almost fainted this morning because it was so infected. He had no choice but to go the hospital."

"Is Dom still at the hospital now? What about Andrew?"

"Dom's out looking for the piece of shit as we speak. He'll kill him if he finds him. Works out well for us, actually."

Davie couldn't understand how calm his brother was being. Hadn't Jordan been his friend? "What do you mean it works out well for us?"

"Because Andrew's a problem that needs dealing with. If Dom gets to him first then we don't have to worry about him coming after us."

"You think that's going to happen? You think Andrew is planning to do the same to us as he did Dom?"

"Seems likely," said Frankie. "The reason Jordan was alone when he got stabbed was that his brother had gone to look for that guy's family – to see if they were still alive and whether or not we'd be facing a murder charge."

"And are we?"

"Yes and no. The girl's okay apparently, but the old dear snuffed it about the same time that Jordan did. Messed up, if you think about it. So you see," said Frankie, "if Dom gets to Andrew first he's doing us all a favour. The police are after his ass, his wife is dead, and he has nothing else left to lose by coming after us."

"He still has a daughter," said Davie, holding on to the fact that they had not taken away absolutely everything from the man.

"Yeah he does," Frankie nodded, "good thinking, little bro. We still have something to use against him if we need to."

"Fuck sake, man." Davie felt like beating the shit out of his brother. If only he could have. "Have you not done enough damage? I can't believe you're still thinking about hurting people."

"Chill the fuck out!"

Davie shoved Frankie hard in the chest. "No, you chill the fuck out. I'm so out of here, man. You can go right to hell for all I care."

Davie turned away from his brother and started walking.

"You get back here right now," Frankie shouted after him. "We need to stick together with that psycho on the loose, you hear me?"

Davie turned back around and started marching back towards his brother. "You don't get it, do you, Frankie? The only psychopath here is you. You belong in jail, man. They should never have let you out"

Frankie pulled out his gun and pointed it in Davie's face.

"Seriously?" Davie shook his head, sighed. "You're pointing that thing at me? You going to shoot your own brother now?"

Frankie's face twitched and the movement seemed to tremor down to his hand, which held the revolver unsteadily. In fact his entire body was shaking.

"Just do it," Davie ordered. "I don't give a fuck anymore."

Frankie's face contorted, the veins in his neck bulged like worms beneath his skin. Davie had never seen his brother like this – so close to freaking out. After a few tense seconds, Frankie chose to lower the weapon. Tears glistened in his eyes, but he did not speak.

Davie had nothing to say either. He started walking away again.

Frankie shouted after him. "I don't want you to get hurt, Davie."

"Don't worry about it," he replied over his shoulder. "You gave me a gun. If I'm in danger I'll take a leaf out of your book and start killing people."

"Where are you going to go?"

Davie thought about it. Then said: "Home."

Frankie followed after him, footsteps keeping time with his own. "That's the first place Andrew will look for us."

Davie turned back around and shrugged. "Then I'll have to deal with the consequences. It's not as though we didn't cause trouble at his house, is it? We deserve whatever we get."

"Why the hell you care so much about this guy?"

"Because if I didn't care then I would be the same as you, and I never want that. Never." Davie could tell he had hurt Frankie with those final words – the silence told him so – but no way did he fucking care.

"Do what the fuck you want," Frankie said finally. "But if I go down I'm taking you with me – and you won't last ten minutes inside."

Davie laughed. "I think that's actually something to be proud of. I'm glad I'm not cut out for prison – means I'm still a human being and not an animal."

For the first time in his life, Davie turned his back on his big brother.

-25-

Andrew had no clue what he planned on doing, but he had lost none of his motivation that he would do something. For all he knew, he could be walking towards a house full of druggies, carrying knives even nastier than the one he currently had hidden on his person. The house was large, posh even, and certainly not what Andrew had been expecting.

I guess crime really does pay.

Before he even had a chance to complete his walk along the path, the front door opened and a topless young man stood in the opening.

"The hell are you?" the youth demanded.

"I'm looking for Frankie."

"Join the club."

Andrew didn't understand. "Do you know where I can find him?"

The youth, that Andrew surmised must be Damien, stepped out onto the pavement to meet him. "You're the guy that has a beef with him, ain't ya?"

Andrew raised his arm slightly; ready to grab the knife stuffed into his waistband at the slightest hint of a threat. "I guess you could say that?"

Damien grinned. "Well, I hope you fuck him up. He has it coming."

Andrew frowned. "Huh?"

"Frankie jacked some of my shit earlier. He ain't a friend of mine anymore."

Andrew attempted a nervous smile. It seemed appropriate in the moment to show friendliness. The enemy of my enemy is my friend. "T-that's...good to hear. So do you know where I can find him?"

Damien shrugged. "Honestly, I don't, mate. If I knew, I would tell you, honestly. What he done to your family is messed up. How are they?"

"My wife is dead." Andrew would allow no emotion into his voice as he spoke. He could not afford to be weak right now.

Damien shook his head and seemed genuinely disgusted. "That prick has a goddamn screw loose."

Andrew sensed an opportunity to get answers. "Is that why he did this to me? Because he's crazy?"

"Dunno. Maybe. Knowing Frankie, it could just be because he don't like your face..." Damien's words trailed off for a minute and a realisation seemed to dawn on his face. "You know, now that I'm looking at you..."

"What?" Andrew asked. "Do I look like someone?"

Damien huffed and shook his head. "Damn, no wonder the guy hates you."

Andrew sensed that Damien was about to say more, but then someone appeared in the doorway behind him.

Anger welled up inside of Andrew and his eyes narrowed. "Michelle?"

Michelle stared out at Andrew and was obviously surprised to see him, her badly bruised jaw hanging agape. Then she turned angry. Running at Andrew, she screamed, "You killed Jordan, you bastard."

Andrew sidestepped and shoved out at her. The girl went flying into the grass on her hands and knees.

"I assume you two have met, then?" Damien quipped from the doorway.

Andrew turned to him. "You going to get involved in this?"

"She made her own bed. She can fucking well lie in it." Damien started to close the door, but halfway he stopped and gave Andrew some parting advice. "Hey, man, watch yourself with Frankie, okay? The stuff he jacked from me, it was a pair of shooters."

"Guns?" Andrew attempted to clarify, but Damien had already closed the door and turned off the hallway light.

"You fucker." Michelle cursed more obscenities at him as she clambered to her feet. She was half-naked and muddy, covered only by a pair of linen shorts and a strappy top. Her nakedness didn't seem to bother her, though, and she launched another attack. Striking out like a seasoned pugilist, Andrew struck her ribs. She fell back to the ground, sucking in air.

"How's that feel, sweetheart? I got a blade in my ribs so you still have a ways to go before you know about real pain." He kicked her, striking her ribs again in the same exact spot. Her girl's cheeks turned bright red and she struggled to catch a single breath.

"Hurts, doesn't it? Now imagine if I put you through this for hours on end, or made you watch while I tortured your family." He kicked her again, this time in her rump. He felt his foot impact with the pointed tip of her tailbone and she squealed in agony.

"I'm sorry," she screamed at him, finally managing to find her breath. "Just leave me alone...please."

Andrew looked down at the pathetic, mud-covered girl and felt no remorse. She was as twisted and as evil as Frankie. In fact, she had delighted in his family's misery more than anyone else. "Seriously?" he asked her. "You're going to beg me? Did I not beg you? Did you listen when I pleaded?"

Michelle shook her head. Tears smudged her makeup in the same way Penelope's had the evening before. Andrew struck out again, kicking her face as hard as he could, and enjoying the feeling of several of her teeth cracking in her jaw as he knocked her cold. But as much as the hatred filled his heart and encased his grieving soul, Andrew did not possess the ability to beat a young girl to death – regardless of how much she might deserve it.

So Andrew knocked on Damien's door and waited for it to open again. When it did, he nodded to the lad and said, "I need to borrow something."

***

It took only minutes to carry Michelle into a nearby wood. Luckily Damien's street was upmarket and lined with small outcroppings of woodland. It was frightening that nobody noticed Andrew abduct the girl, but it wasn't something he was going to complain about right now.

Andrew knelt beside the girl as she lay propped up against a gnarled oak tree. She was an unconscious mess. While she'd been sleeping, Andrew used the scissors he'd borrowed from Damien to completely remove her hair, humiliating her in the same way she and her friends had done to Pen. It still wasn't sufficient punishment for what she'd done, but Andrew hoped it was enough to teach her a lesson.

He slapped at her cheeks to wake her up, harder than he needed to because the act itself felt so satisfying. After half-a-dozen blows, it finally worked. Her lids fluttered and her eyeballs rolled forwards from the back of her head. She looked content, like coming out of a pleasant dream, but then her consciousness returned to reality and she saw Andrew leaning over her. She panicked.

"Help me. Please, somebody."

Andrew slapped her face again, harder than he had done to wake her. Instantly, she stopped screaming. "Shut up, girl. I won't hurt you if you tell me what I want."

Michelle's eyes were round and white like a frightened animal's. Her words came out hurried and short of breath. "Tell you...what?"

Andrew leant closer to her, their noses almost touching. "Where's Frankie?" he growled.

"I...I don't know."

Andrew pulled the knife from his belt and held it to her face, pressing it beneath her left eye. "Don't make me ask you again."

"Please...please...I really don't know. Damien said Frankie left his place a few hours ago before I even got there. Frankie doesn't know I was with Damien."

Andrew huffed. "You really are a piece of work, aren't you?"

"Please don't tell him."

Andrew couldn't believe it. The girl's level of self-importance was astounding. "Do you think I give a damn about your love life? You can screw half of England for all I care. I just want Frankie. Besides I don't think he'd like you now that you've cut your hair."

Michelle slapped both hands to her head and squealed when she felt nothing but scalp and random thickets of hair. Before she had time to lose herself to hysteria, Andrew slapped her again. He didn't have time to watch her self-pity.

"Tell me where Frankie is, or you'll lose more than just your hair."

"I-I don't know where he is." She was pleading now and, regrettably, Andrew was inclined to believe her. He was confident that he'd rattled her enough that she wouldn't dare lie to him. She had no idea where Frankie was.

He removed the knife from beneath her eye, dragging it downwards so that it bit slightly at her flesh and drew blood. He ignored her flinches of pain and made his next demand. "Tell me where you think Frankie would go. Home, maybe?"

Michelle laughed. "That's the last place you'll find him. He's never there if he can help it. I know where you can find Dom, though."

Andrew took a breath and held it. He hadn't thought as much about the rest of Frankie's crew, but they were due just as much punishment as he was. He had already dealt with Jordan, so why not pay his brother a visit too? At the very least there was a good chance that Dom could lead him closer to Frankie.

"Okay," said Andrew. "Tell me where to find Dom."

-26-

Davie stood at his front door not wanting to go in. The thought of facing his mother after the previous night's events was more than he could handle. There would be a lecture about staying out at all hours just waiting for him. It was the very least of what he deserved, but his soul felt so brittle right now that the slightest knock could shatter him like a pane of glass. He needed sleep and nothing else.

Davie turned the handle. The door was not locked because his mother never left the house. As long as she had beer – and sons to fetch it for her – then there was no reason to ever face the outside world. He stepped inside and the smell of that very same beer filled his nostrils.

His mother heard the door open and shouted out from the living room. "Davie, is that you? Get in here."

Davie sighed and passed from the hallway into the next room. His mother was sprawled on the couch in her nightshirt and slippers, trying to pull herself up to a sitting position but failing pathetically. Davie moved over to help her up. She declined his hand and continued to struggle. Eventually she made it upright and immediately began to glower at him.

"Where have you been?"

"I was out with Frankie."

His mother spat. The drool landed on her nightshirt. "Frankie? I told you to stay away from that wretch."

"I know," Davie admitted. "I will from now on, mum, I promise."

His mother stared at him some more, trying to focus her eyes as she swayed to and fro, seemed totally unaware that a bandage adorned his head. "Lies." She slurred in his face. "Don't you lie to me, boy."

"I'm not. I saw what he's really like last night. I want no more to do with him."

"Why? What happened? What did you boys do? I best not have the police around here. I have enough to cope with."

"Nothing happened, mum. I just found out that he wasn't a very nice person."

She took a swig of beer and laughed. "He's been no good since the day I shat him out."

Davie was weary and his usual tolerance for his mother's bile was absent. He said, "Maybe Frankie wouldn't have turned out so bad if you'd been a better mother."

Predictably, his drunken mother went nuclear. She threw her empty beer can at Davie, hitting his face above the eyebrow. "How dare you, you little swine. I give you a home and feed you, and this is how you repay me? Twenty years of my life down the pan for you boys. I've a right mind to kick you both out."

"You wouldn't do that," Davie said calmly."

"Oh, wouldn't I? We'll see about that, you ungrateful brat."

"You won't throw us out, because you'd lose all your benefits and won't be able to drink yourself stupid every day. As for putting a roof over your head, the government only gives it to you because of me. You'd be in a flat somewhere if I were to ever leave here, so I don't want to hear any more of your selfish complaining. The only person to blame for your terrible life is you, so deal with it." He reached down to the floor and picked up the empty beer can that she had thrown at him. He tossed it back onto her lap. "And you can get your own beer from now on. Go outside and let the whole world see what you are."

Davie's mother unleashed a tirade of abuse, but he was already out the door and halfway up the stairs before she managed to complete her first slurred sentence. It was just background noise. Standing up to her her should've left him elated, but it didn't. There was too much on his mind to enjoy a pointless victory over his mother. After what he and his brother had put Andrew and his family through, there was no room for any emotion aside from shame and regret.

Nothing will ever make up for what they did.

Davie entered the cramped space of his bedroom and hopped up onto his unmade bed. What chance had he and Frankie had growing up with their mother as their moral guardian? Ending up in a young offender's home had probably been inevitable from the moment Frankie was born, and Davie was heading the same way. He thought about what Damien had said about his brother's time in prison and felt sick. Frankie was strong. The thought of him being...being helplessly abused did not mesh with the image that Davie held of him. It made his heart hurt just trying to consider it.

Even if it was true, what difference did it make? Frankie was broken and there was no way to fix him. Understanding a monster doesn't change the fact that it's still a monster. Davie had looked into his brother's eyes and saw something missing. Was it compassion?

Did that mean Frankie was evil?

No, Davie told himself, he's my brother and he doesn't deserve the existence he's been given. His whole life he's looked out for me. Now it's my turn to look out for him.

Davie hopped off his bed and took a deep breath, reached into his pocket and pulled out the revolver Frankie had given him.

-27-

The Trumpet bar and lounge was located in a rough housing estate opposite a rundown supermarket and failing video store. Andrew had never been here before but had heard enough stories to suggest that drinking here was only for a certain kind of individual.

He took the first of the crumbling stone steps leading up to the pub's entrance and prepared himself to go inside. The lights were on and a flickering glow gave away the presence of a natural fire. The thought of all that warmth welcomed Andrew in from the evening's icy rain and hastened his approach. Once inside, he saw that the pub was almost empty, and it took several seconds to even spot a single soul. There was a slender brunette restocking crisps behind the bar and a dishevelled old man sitting opposite with a half-empty pint of bitter in front of him.

Andrew moved up beside the old man and took the stool next to him.

"A new face," said the barmaid. "Don't get many of those around here. I'm Steph and this wrinkly fart we call Old Graham."

"You cheeky mare," the old man replied but was laughing.

"Pleased to meet you," said Andrew. He slid a ten-pound note across the counter. "Top the fella up and one for yourself. Mine's a lager."

Steph smiled. "Very generous of you."

"Yes," said Old Graham. "You're my kind of man."

"Then perhaps you could help me with something."

The old man received his pint from the barmaid and took a sip of it. Then, as the barmaid went off to pour the next one, he turned to Andrew. "Okay. What do you need?"

"Kid called Dom."

The old man raised his greying eyebrows in a look of understanding. "Black guy. A twin, yeah?"

"Not anymore," Andrew replied, "but, yeah. Do you know him?"

"Not really but I've seen him and his brother in here on the few odd occasions. Played a game of pool with him once before the old table got smashed up in a bar fight.

"Has he been here tonight?"

The old man shrugged. "I've only just got here, pal."

"He left about ten minutes ago," said Steph, coming back with the second pint Andrew had ordered from her. "Hit the booze pretty hard for an hour or so, then went on his way."

"Do you know where he went?"

Steph shook her head. "Never said more than a couple words to me the whole time he was here. What you want with him anyway?"

"I'm going to kill him." He let the words linger in the air for a moment and realised that he had shocked the others into silence. Maybe they didn't think he was serious, so he elaborated. "And I'm going to do it tonight."

"What for?" she asked, glancing around nervously.

"Because, last night, Dom helped murder my wife and put my daughter in the hospital. He did it for kicks."

Steph stared at him hard. She was trying to work him out, to see if he was serious or just one of the regular whackos who were par for the course of a barmaid's job.

"You really don't know where he went?" Andrew asked.

Steph shook her head. "I'm sorry. Even if I did know, I wouldn't help you commit murder."

Andrew understood and thanked her anyway, got off his stool and began to walk away. He stopped when Old Graham reached out and touched him.

"Are you telling the truth? He hurt your family?"

Andrew nodded.

"What are you doing, Graham?" Steph hissed from behind the bar.

The old man sighed back at her, but continued talking with Andrew. "I don't know where he was heading, pal, but he took a phone call just before he left. I didn't hear most of what he was saying – he was upset and angry – but I did hear him say something about a hospital."

Andrew's stomach turned. Jordan was dead, which meant his brother, Dom, would have only one reason to visit the hospital. He was going after Bex. Payback. The person on the phone had probably been Frankie, egging him friend on and eager to have a potential witness dealt with.

Andrew swallowed. He had to get there first.

He turned back to the bar and looked at Steph. "Dom's going after my daughter. Please, call the hospital and tell them that Rebecca Goodman is in danger. Rebecca Goodman, okay?"

She just stood there, befuddled.

Andrew shouted at her. "Rebecca Goodman. Make the call."

Then he turned and fled, barging through the pub's main door. The rain had gotten ferocious in the short time he'd been inside the pub and it hit his skin now with enough force to sting.

He stopped at the bottom of the pub's steps and allowed himself a second to consider his options. He needed to get to the hospital as quickly as possible, but was at least two miles away with no car. There was a bus route nearby but he had no idea how regular it was or even where it went. A taxi would be the quickest option but he'd still have to wait for it to arrive, and he couldn't take the risk of it turning up late. There was only one solution that seemed viable. He had to make it back home and get in his car.

He took off running. Breathlessness came quickly, forcing a stitch into his side that merged with the pain of the stab wound in his calf, but he had to keep going. Every second was a second that Bex might not have.

He ran as fast as his legs would take him, his chest near bursting.

But he kept going, never slowing down for a single second.

One street away from his own, and he was finally forced to slow down to a jog, the pain in his ribs growing to a point where it threatened to drop him to the floor unconscious. When he placed a hand against his side, he discovered blood seeping from the shallow knife wound where Michelle had stuck him. It was hot and sticky as it trickled down his skin.

But there was no time to wallow. He put aside the pain and drew from reserves he never knew he possessed, and managed to round the final corner at full speed. His car was right in front of him, exactly where he had left it on the curb beside the house. For some irrational reason he had dreaded it would not be there. Thank God that it was.

Don't worry, Bex. I'm coming.

He reached the Mercedes and skidded to a halt beside the driver's side, fumbling in his pocket for the keys.

"You're dead, motherfucker?"

Andrew turned around just in time to see a fist coming at his face. It connected with his jaw and sent his eyes rolling back in his head; and when he came to, he found himself in the dark.

***

There was no space to move. Every time Andrew tried to straighten out an arm or leg he hit against the walls of his confinement. His head was spinning and a wicked lump throbbed on the side of his head, making it extremely hard to think. It wasn't until after several minutes of being curled up in the dark, listening to a nearby mechanical humming, that he realised he was inside a car.

I'm locked in the boot.

Andrew could tell by the sound of the engine that it was his own car. Dom must have grabbed the keys from him after throwing his knockout punch. Now Andrew was a hostage on his way to God knows where.

He felt about himself for a solution, but struggled to find anything at all beside his own body. If he remembered correctly, the only things inside the boot was a jacket belonging to Pen and a handheld vacuum cleaner – neither would do anything to help him escape. There was a tool kit, too, but it was hidden in a compartment beneath the shelf he was lying on. He did the only thing he could think of, and kicked out with both legs as hard as he could.

The plastic mouldings of the car's luggage compartment bent under the assault, but behind that was unmovable steel from the vehicle's chassis. He had nowhere near enough strength to kick his way out and every time he tried his calf cried out in pain. His whole body cried out.

Something occurred to him then. He still had his kitchen knife; could feel it digging into his side. He pulled it free of his waistband and unrolled it from the tea towel. He may have had no way to escape, but at least he had a weapon to use when Dom opened the boot. If it was, in fact, Dom who was driving the car.

As if reading his mind, the car began to slow down, the growl of the engine deepening as the revs lowered. Andrew gripped the knife tightly.

The car came to a full stop and jolted as the handbrake was applied by its operator. Andrew's body tensed like a coiled spring as he listened to the driver open his door and step out. The weight of the car shifted, rocking back and forth before settling again. The ground crunched beneath the feet of the driver. The footsteps approached the boot.

Andrew waited.

Seconds passed by.

The boot did not open.

His nose picked up the scent of something – something acrid, gaseous. His ears picked up the sound of liquid, splashing and pouring.

His mind put the two things together.

Petrol.

Mortal fear seized Andrew. He had resigned himself to the possibility of dying tonight, but being burned alive was not something he could bear.

He kicked out at the boot's lid and screamed out, trying to reason with the person attempting to burn him alive. It was no use; the petrol continued to pour, seeping through the gaps in the vehicle's bodywork and onto Andrew's clothing. His eyes began to sting. He tried to figure a way out before it was too late, frantically clawing at his surroundings. Each of the four walls was flat and featureless – nothing to grab hold of – but eventually his hands caught against something above. It was the locking mechanism for the boot. He fiddled with the contraption but could make no sense of it in the dark. All he could think to do was stab at it with his knife. The blade lodged into the plastic covering and stuck. He pulled it out and stabbed again. Again.

Petrol continued to soak through into the boot.

Andrew kept on stabbing, harder and harder.

Eventually, part of the casing began to come away, revealing the lock fittings inside. Andrew reached his frantic fingers into the gap and snatched at anything he could find in the dark. He pulled and prodded hoping beyond all hope to find a way out.

Something clicked.

A sliver of light entered the boot space and Andrew felt his heart leap into his chest. The person outside was still busy pouring petrol and didn't seem to notice that the boot lid had opened a couple of inches.

Warily, Andrew edged the boot open further. He could see someone's legs through the widening gap, lit by the car's headlamps. With a depp breath, held long enough to make his lungs ache, Andrew unleashed himself, uncoiling out of the boot like a striking cobra. His head and shoulders hit the lid and forced it open while his legs sprung and launched him into the air. He came down on his attacker and the two of them tumbled to the floor. Andrew lost his knife in the scuffle, but wasn't deterred. He kicked out at his attacker, which did turn out to be Dom. The teenager rolled over onto his side, cursing in pain and anger.

Andrew glanced around and considered making a run for it. They were in a wood, and the cold rain mixed with the late hour made the area seem menacing. If he ran, he would probably end up lost and he couldn't afford for that to happen. Bex might still need him – there was still Davie and Frankie to think about. Dom could be intending to keep Andrew away.

"I'm going to kill you," said Dom, rising to his feet, jeans covered in mud.

Andrew snarled. "Going to have to disagree with you there, blud."

Dom rushed forward like a wild bull, and even snorted like one. Andrew met the charge head on and the two collided in a brawl, fists flying. Dom landed a couple of blows on Andrew's chin, but Andrew was too determined, and prepared to fight dirty. He jammed his thumb into Dom's eye.

Dom reeled backwards, swiping out blindly with both hands. Andrew seized the advantage and advanced, grabbing the youth around the throat and kicking the legs out from under him. Dom hit the dirt on his back, twigs snapping beneath him, and Andrew followed him right down to the floor, still squeezing at his throat, bearing down with all of his weight.

Dom struggled and clawed, but it was useless. The fear in his eyes dulled as his cheeks swelled and seemed to turn purple in the harsh glare of the car's headlights, just seconds away from passing on to the next life.

A knife appeared and embedded itself in Andrew's face. The blade entered his cheek and protruded into his mouth, slicing his tongue. He released his grip on Dom's throat and grabbed the blade's handle hysterically. He yanked it back out of his face and screamed. Blood filled his mouth and made him choke.

Dom made it up to his knees, wheezing and spluttering as his windpipe recovered from being constricted to the point of near-asphyxia.

Andrew was in no state to launch another attack. Shudders wracked his body and his mind kept trying to spin into unconsciousness. If that happened he was as good as dead – Dom would slit his throat while he was sleeping. Yet, even with his face torn up and bleeding, Andrew was still the one with the upper hand. He had Dom's knife now. The small rubber handle gripped tightly in his hand.

But Andrew couldn't get to his feet. He crawled forwards on his hands and knees, attempting to reach Dom before the boy managed to recover.

When Dom saw Andrew approaching with the knife, he scrambled to his feet and took off in a panic. Andrew gave all that he had and managed to get up and take off after him.

Dom was quick, but he was winded and half-blind from a gouged eye. He had to feel his way through the trees in the dark. Every now and then, he would stumble against a branch or trip over a root. Andrew was closing the distance. The deciding factor now would be stamina. Andrew's lungs were burning and his stomach was paving the way for an onslaught of retching. He wasn't cut out for so much exertion on a good day, let alone with a stab wound in his face, calf, and ribs.

But he couldn't quit. As long as he had control over his legs he was going to keep going. He dodged between skeletal trees and fallen logs. His legs pumped like pistons; his breath came out in gasps. Dom was losing steam, legs getting heavier, strides shortening. The gap between them quickly decreased.

Dom was only an arm's reach away. Just a few more steps. Andrew timed his strides and prepared to pounce. He sprung forward and managed to grab hold of the boy's sweatshirt. Dom's legs tangled together and he tripped onto his face, sliding in the dirt. Andrew hopped aside and came to a stop beside him. Standing over the boy, he readied himself to use the knife and finish the job.

He pointed the knife at Dom's throat. "Where's Frankie?" His words were slurred, mouth still full of blood. "Where is he?"

"Fuck you man," Dom spat, but he made no attempt to fight. He was beaten.

Andrew could hear the fear in the boy's voice. "Do you want to die, Dom? Do you want me to gut you like your brother?"

"Shut up. Go...go to hell." He was sobbing now.

Andrew exhaled. His lust for blood deflated as he saw the childish mess at his feet. "Look. I don't need to hurt you, Dom. I've already taken what you've taken from me, so we're even. I just want Frankie. Where is he?"

Dom sneered and seemed to get back some of his swagger. "He at the hospital, doing yo daughter like yo did my bro."

Thinking about it filled Andrew with more terror than he could hold inside of himself, but he couldn't afford to lose control. He had to remain focused. "Do you have a mobile phone on you, Dom?"

"Course I do."

"Then use it," Andrew swiped the knife and cut a furrow in the boy's cheek making him hiss. "Make a call or I'll open you up and leave you to bleed to death."

"A call to who?"

Andrew booted Dom in his side. "Who do you think, idiot? Frankie. Call him and say that if he doesn't leave the hospital right now to meet me, I'll slice your throat like a chicken."

"Okay, okay." Dom made the call on a small black phone that he plucked from his jean pockets. He waited a few moments until someone on the other end answered. "Hey, man. You gotta come get me. That motherfucking psycho has got me at knifepoint, yo. I'm lying in the mud like a sucker and he's gunna slice me like he did Jordan if you don't come get me."

There was silence in the woods for almost a full minute while Dom listened to Frankie's reply. The whole time Andrew stood and watched Dom's face. It seemed to grow grimmer with each passing second. Eventually Dom finished the call and put the phone away, then looked up at Andrew. "Bitch put the phone down on me."

Andrew had a bad feeling. Why wouldn't Frankie help his friend? "What did he say?"

Dom shook his head and seemed mortified. "He said, I should deal with my own shit, and if I was a man I should take you out for what you done to my bro."

Andrew sniffed. "Want to try it, homie?"

Dom put his hands up. "No man, enough."

"Did Frankie say where he is?"

Dom nodded but seemed like he didn't want to answer. "The hospital. Apparently there're pigs about, so he's lying low, waiting for the coast to clear"

The barmaid must have done as I asked her and called the hospital. Thank you, Steph.

The police would buy Andrew some time. He could still make it to the hospital if he hurried back to his car, but first he needed to find out exactly where he was.

"What is this place?" he asked Dom.

"The woods at the back of Brockhill Farm."

Andrew knew it. It was a rural plot of fields and woodland on the edge of town; a mile away from the nearest built-up area. Great place to murder someone.

"I ought to leave you here to die," said Andrew. "But you're too pathetic to waste my time on."

Dom seemed to recover some of his lost confidence. Obviously he'd been expecting Andrew to kill him and was relieved to hear otherwise. "This shit ain't over, man. I respect you letting me live right now, but if Frankie doesn't finish you then I will."

"Please try. Then I'll have an excuse to send you to your brother."

It was likely to be a very bad idea leaving Dom alive, but Andrew would be in jail soon and unreachable for quests of revenge. Besides, he couldn't kill someone cowering at his feet – he wasn't that man, even after what he had become. Dom's brother was dead and hopefully that was enough retribution to allow Andrew to sleep at night.

He left Dom lying in the dirt and crunched his way back through the gloomy wood, trying to get his bearings. Thankfully, it wasn't long before he saw the headlights of his car, lighting up the rain as it fell in thick sheets.

With the engine still running, the keys would be inside, so Andrew wasted no time in heading for the driver's side and hopping in. He slammed the door shut and glanced out of the windscreen. Dom was back on his feet, but made no attempt to stop Andrew.

It wasn't clear which direction the road was, so Andrew decided to manoeuvre the car around, between the trees, until he was facing in the opposite direction, then set off in a straight line, hoping that it would turn out to be the route Dom had taken them in on.

The automatic wipers came on and Andrew had to squint to see. There were trees everywhere and it was a real effort to avoid them all in the darkness and rain. Several times Andrew had to brake sharply and make erratic steering movements. The uneven, bumpy ground didn't help much either and the tyres barely kept their grip in the sliding mud.

Eventually the trees began to thin in number and opened out into a clearing. The car hit a water-logged field and the steering got even heavier. Andrew clutched the steering wheel tighter and leant forward to examine his surroundings. The field stretched down a hill and was lined on all sides by a wooden beamed fence. In the distance was the easily distinguishable lights of a house.

Most likely the Brockhill estate.

Andrew knew that the large Manor on the edge of town was roadside. If he headed for the building and it did turn out to be Brockhill Estate then he could get back onto a main road and head back into town. He would reach the hospital in fifteen minutes.

Andrew put his foot down and the car careened down the hill. As the house below became clearer into view, it revealed itself to be just the building he was hoping for. Andrew wouldn't have to cover the entire distance to Brockhill Manor because there was a steel gate about fifty-metres up from it at the edge of the field. The gate was hanging open, obviously left that way by Dom. Beyond it: the main road.

Andrew gripped the steering wheel tighter and sped up. I'm coming, Bex. Just hold on.

-28-

Davie tried calling his brother several times but there was no answer. Same thing when he made a call to Dom. He began to worry. Frankie had been unstable before all this shit that had happened, but now he was borderline insane. Still, Davie forgave his brother's faults now, even if he couldn't come fully to terms with them. He was determined to put a stop to the situation before it could escalate further. There was still a chance for Frankie to retain some shred of humanity – if he were to just stop now.

No more people needed to get hurt.

Davie's biggest concern right now was that Frankie would try and finish what he'd started by going after Andrew and his family again. He'd already made suggestions that he needed to deal with any loose ends.

The first place Davie tried was Andrew's home – it was a possibility that Frankie would return there to resume his beef with the man – but as he rounded the corner, Davie saw that the house's lights were out and that – even more tellingly – Andrew's Mercedes was gone from its space at the side of the road. No one was home. Davie started thinking about Plan B.

If Frankie were still looking for trouble, he'd be headed wherever Andrew was. So where was Andrew?

There was, of course, only one place Andrew would be. Davie had seen how much the man loved his family and there was no doubt that he would be at his daughter's bedside.

Which meant Frankie as probably at the hospital.

Davie jingled with the change in his pocket. There was a bus stop nearby that went not too far from the hospital. If a bus came soon then Davie could be there within the next half an hour. He just hoped it would be soon enough.

He reached the bus stop at the end of the road and waited. The act of doing nothing was frustrating. Every part of his body urged for action but, with no other way of getting to the hospital, Davie had no choice but to wait. He concentrated on the noise of the heavy rain hitting the curved tin roof of the shelter before sliding off in sheets. Somehow, the sound managed to calm him slightly – enough that when the bus finally arrived, Davie didn't notice at first.

"You getting in or what?" asked the bus driver, snapping Davie out of his daze.

Davie looked up, startled, and then nodded. "Sorry. Had my mind on other things."

"Nothing bad I hope?"

Davie stepped onto the bus and gave the driver his change. "I would settle for bad, right now. Things are way beyond that."

The driver frowned at him. "Well, keep your chin up lad. Got your whole life ahead of you."

Davie moved to take a seat as the hydraulic doors pumped closed behind him. He sat down and waited. He would be at the hospital soon.

He just hoped it would be in time.

-29-

Andrew parked his car at the rear of the hospital. It meant it would take longer to reach Bex, but he couldn't risk running into any police that might be at the entrance. Wardsley and Dalton may have been on his side, but they were not the only officers likely to be at the hospital and, as a man wanted for murder, he was certain that a description of both him and his car would have been issued to the entire local force.

Andrew moved between cars, glancing forward, left and right for any law enforcement. Sure enough, there was a plain-clothes officer at the entrance to A and E. Andrew could tell the man was with the police by the stiff way he was standing and by the regular tilts of his head. The man was speaking into a microphone on his collar.

Andrew stayed to the edge of the car park and headed around the side of the hospital to look for a less conspicuous entrance. There was a fire exit near the rear of the building and it was open – a member of staff standing in front of it with a cigarette. Andrew approached with his head down, not wanting to draw attention.

"Hey, man, you can't come through here. Use the front."

Andrew looked up and smiled. The man was wearing chef's whites and obviously worked in the hospital's canteen. Bex's room wasn't far from the canteen.

"You mind if I just sneak through? I won't tell anybody."

The man shook his head. "You need to use the front entrance. What you doing around here anyway? And what the hell is with your face?"

Andrew had to think fast. He'd totally forgotten that half his face was ripped to pieces. He must look like an extra from a zombie-movie. "Trying to avoid my mother-in-law," he said out of nowhere. "My wife and I have been in a car accident. Her mother just turned up to see her. I was out the front having a fag when I saw her heading my way. I dashed around the back because I don't want to have to deal with her right now. She's a total bitch and I know she'll blame me for the crash. In fact I blame myself."

The chef stared Andrew in the face, trying to work him out. Andrew stared right back, sweat beading on his forehead.

"Okay," the man said eventually. "I hear you. My mother-in-law is a dragon too."

Andrew thanked the man and went to walk past, but didn't make it through without being stopped first. "There a problem?" he asked.

The chef shook his head. "Just wondered if you had a spare cigarette. This is my last one."

Of course Andrew didn't. He didn't really smoke...but that's was what he had told the chef he was doing there.

Andrew shook his head. "Sorry, mate. I just smoked my last as well. Need to go the gift shop soon as the old witch leaves."

The chef nodded and laughed. "No worries, man. Hope your wife recovers."

Andrew patted the man on the back. "Thanks. Guess I'll go get my face stitched up while she's with her mum."

Andrew made it through into a hallway. As he'd expected, he was near the hospital canteen. If he remembered correctly, Bex was a couple of wards down. Without interference he would be there in minutes.

But there was going to be police. What would he do then?

Andrew decided he was happy to be arrested if it meant seeing that Bex was okay and that Frankie was not nearby. He could tell the police that Bex was in danger and they would protect her. At the start of the night he'd been set on murder – on ending Frankie's life – but right now all that mattered was his daughter's safety. Revenge was something that would have to take a backseat. Whether he liked it or not, he had no choice but to leave Frankie's fate in the hands of the courts. At least he'd made the rest of them pay.

He kept his back close to the wall as he progressed down the corridors. He may have been willing to get caught by the police, but not until he saw that Bex was okay. He followed the signs for Ward 7 – he was sure that was the right one.

The hallways up ahead were busier, and doctors milled about casually while nurses rushed around them. They weren't quite the hectic, overly-stressed members of staff from A and E, but seemed agitated all the same. A sign hanging from the ceiling read: RECOVERY WARDS.

Andrew reached the end of the corridor and looked around the corner. His heart skipped three beats when he saw the police officers standing there. They were gathered around a single room.

It must have been Bex's room.

So close. So goddamn close.

Andrew leant back against the wall and beat his head against the cement. The pounding actually helped him think, dulling the pain that seemed to emanate from a dozen different places on his body. He had to find a way to get the officers away. Andrew couldn't risk Frankie sneaking in and hurting his daughter while the police were busy arresting him.

Looking around, Andrew noticed something that could offer a solution. On the wall, only a few feet away, was a small red panel with a film of glass at its centre. Written in ominous white font were the words: PRESS IN CASE OF FIRE.

There was no fire but Andrew wasted no time in pressing his thumb against the glass panel. It compressed within its red metal surroundings and a shrill alarm pierced the air. Andrew glanced back around the corner and watched the confusion percolate amongst the staff and members of the public. Even better, Andrew watched while a nurse walked up to the police officers and insisted that they left the ward along with everyone else. It didn't look like they were very willing but, thankfully, the nurse was persistent. Then something that did not occur to Andrew started to happen. Orderlies started to appear in great numbers and went about wheeling away the patients from their wards. Andrew felt stupid that it hadn't occurred to him that the whole hospital would be evacuated, patients and all – not just the staff.

Andrew watched while a young male orderly entered Bex's room to bring her out. Andrew made his move. He dashed across the nurse's area, dodging between preoccupied men and women that were unaware that the fire was only fictitious. He hopped out of the way of an oncoming gurney, shoes skidding on the polished floor, and then managed to barrel his body over to Bex's room. He was just about to open the door when someone grabbed him from the side.

"Andrew."

Andrew spun around with his fist raised, but lowered it when he saw it was Officer Dalton.

"You need to come with me," she told him. "I take it the fire alarm was your doing?"

"I just need to see my daughter and then I'll come with you."

Dalton shook her head. "I can't allow it. There's police looking everywhere for you. I can't risk anyone witnessing me doing anything other than taking you in. I already gave you the chance to do what you needed to do. Now you need to keep your promise and come with me, Andrew."

"Please," he pleaded. "Just let me say goodbye to my daughter. You can wait right outside the door.

Once again Andrew managed to get the female officer to relent. Her face softened and she actually seemed annoyed at herself for being so soft. "Just don't make me regret this, Andrew. I've already put my life in jeopardy for you."

Andrew put his hand on the door to enter, but Dalton put a hand on his chest and stopped him.

"Frankie?"

Andrew looked her in the eye and shook his head solemnly. "I couldn't find him."

He turned away and pushed open the door, before stepping inside. The first thing he saw was Bex lying in her bed. The second was the orderly lying unconscious on the floor. The third thing Andrew saw was Frankie pointing a gun at his face.

"Glad you could finally join us," Frankie snarled. "It's time to wrap this shit up."

-30-

Andrew stared down the barrel of the gun – something he never thought he'd ever find himself doing. Guns were completely outlawed in the United Kingdom, and he'd never seen one for real, but here he was now, close enough to smell the oil on the metal.

"Daddy?"

Bex was terrified and Andrew didn't want her to see that he was too. "It's okay, sweetie," he told her. "We'll get this all worked out."

"I hear you had a little run in with Dom?" said Frankie. "Right after you killed his bro. That was cold, man." His face twitched manically as he spoke.

Andrew put both hands up. It felt like the appropriate thing to do. "There's a police officer right outside the door. Just give yourself up and there's a chance you might not spend your entire life in jail."

Frankie laughed. "Not going to happen. Got business to deal with first – but hey, why leave your little police officer friend waiting outside? Bring her in to join the fun."

Andrew lowered his hands and raised his eyebrows. "What are you talking about?"

Frankie motioned at the door with his revolver. "Tell her to get in here, but don't make it obvious what's going on."

"No," said Andrew in a firm voice. He would not bring anybody else into his mess. Dalton had already done enough for him.

Frankie pointed the gun at Bex. "I ain't asking, Andrew. Unless you want me to make an entrance in your daughter's forehead, I'd do as you're told."

Andrew sighed. "Officer Dalton. I'm ready to go with you. Would you come in here?"

There was a moment of silence before the officer replied from outside. "No. I think you should come out here."

Frankie shook the gun barrel at him. "Think fast, hero. Get her in here or your daughter's head becomes a wind tunnel."

Andrew swallowed a lump in his throat and considered his words carefully. "Officer Dalton, my daughter would like to speak to you before you arrest me. She wants you to promise you'll get Frankie for what he's done and that you will keep me safe."

Frankie laughed. "Nice."

The door opened and Dalton stepped through. "Sweetheart, I promise we'll send the little bastard down..." Her words trailed off as her eyes caught Frankie standing in the corner of the room.

Frankie grinned at her. "Well, hello there, honey. Why don't you sit your fine ass down over there." He motioned with the gun towards a seat. "Do it now, before I start making holes in people."

Dalton let the door close behind her and took a step towards Frankie. "Drop the weapon, Frankie. Drop it right now and no one has to get hurt."

"Don't think you understand who has the power here, luv. I have a gun and you don't."

Dalton continued to stare Frankie down and Andrew noticed her gradually move a hand to her hip, resting it on the belt that ringed her waist. "I won't ask you again," she told Frankie. "Put. The. Weapon. Down."

Frankie's self-assured grin grew wider. "Sit the fuck down, you stupid bitch. You ain't telling no one to do nothing."

Suddenly Dalton reached for something at her belt, clawing at one of the many poaches that lined her waist, but she wasn't quick enough. Frankie pulled the trigger before Andrew could even see what it was she'd been reaching for.

The whole room seemed to explode with sound. Andrew's ears rang and his vision tilted. When it finally returned to normal, Dalton was sprawled out across the floor, a pool of blood spreading beneath her. She was alive, but the gunshot wound in her guts had made a mess and was obviously causing her an unimaginable amount of pain. Bex began screaming from her bed.

Andrew scurried to help Dalton, but Frankie stood in his way, cocking the revolver ready for the next shot. "Stay the-fuck still."

"Let me help her," demanded Andrew.

Frankie shook his head and sneered. "What's to help? She's done."

Andrew looked down at Dalton and disagreed. She was certainly in bad shape, but she was still conscious and moving – dragging herself across the floor and propping herself up against the wall. With medical attention, she would make it through, he was sure, but if things went on much longer her chances would not be so good. Another life hanging in the balance of Frankie's vendetta. Andrew wished his actions had led him down a better path than this.

Frankie prodded Andrew in his injured ribs with the gun barrel making him wince. Frankie prodded him again for good measure. "Sit down on the floor," he ordered. "No more playin'."

Andrew glanced at his daughter who had tears in her eyes. Then he looked away because it hurt too much to see her in pain. He bent his knees and slid himself down onto the floor beside the door and looked over to the adjacent wall at Dalton. She looked right back at him. Her face was pasty, sweat-covered and pale. Blood spilled from her stomach in a steady stream and drenched her clothing.

"Why are you doing this?" Andrew asked Frankie from the floor. "I mean, really? You're going to spend your whole life in jail, and for what? Cus you don't like the look of my face?"

Frankie's face twitched. "I ain't ever going down again. I'll die first."

"So why then? If you never want to go to prison again, why cause trouble the moment you're out?"

"What the fuck else I gunna do? Work at a bank?"

Andrew shrugged his shoulders. "Why not? You could have done a million different things – but instead you choose to murder my wife?"

"Mum?" Bex's eyes went wide. "No, she's not dead. She can't be."

Andrew hadn't meant for his daughter to find out like that and cursed himself for not thinking. Now that she knew, he was unable to console her. Frankie had once again managed to prevent him from looking after his family.

"I'm sorry," Andrew told her. "I didn't find out until after I left you."

Bex mewled like a wounded animal and buried her face in her hands. Andrew turned his stare back to Frankie. "Do you enjoy this? Causing all of this hurt to innocent people?"

"Who says you're innocent?"

Andrew was ready to give up. There was no part of Frankie that had any remorse or understanding. There might have been something there deep beneath the surface that could be gotten at, but Andrew had no idea what it was.

"My daughter is innocent," Andrew stated. "What has she ever done?"

"She belongs to you."

"And what have I done, exactly? Is this all because I didn't buy you a packet of fags?"

Frankie was breathing quickly and his twitch was becoming more regular and erratic. "You needed to learn a lesson."

"What lesson? You know nothing about me?"

"I needed to teach you some respect."

"Why is it so important that some guy you never met respects you? Are you that insecure?"

Frankie thrust the gun forward at Andrew and for a moment it looked like he would pull the trigger again. Andrew didn't flinch though – not for a scumbag like Frankie. When the gun didn't go off, it became clear that Andrew was scratching at something – something beneath Frankie's surface that was heavily guarded.

Andrew smirked, enjoying the sight of Frankie squirming. "But this was never about me, was it? This is about your own bullshit. So what was it, Frankie? Daddy abuse you?"

"Fuck you. I never even knew my Dad."

Andrew was getting close. He could sense it. "Hardly surprising, having met your mother. Maybe it was the young offender's home then? Did one of the bigger boy's make you his bitch?"

Frankie pulled the trigger. Andrew's vision went white like someone had lit a firework inside his skull. The pain came hot and heavy, accompanied by thick waves of nausea and mind-rattling dizziness.

I've been shot. Holy shit, I've been shot.

The pain was so gigantic and all consuming that Andrew couldn't even tell where he'd been hit. It was only when his vision returned, and he saw the blood pouring from his knee, that he knew. The agony was so massive that he knew he'd never walk right again.

If the psychopath didn't kill him altogether.

Bex was screaming again, crying out for her father and begging for Frankie to leave them all alone.

"I told you not to fuck with me," Frankie screamed at Andrew on the floor. "I told you, didn't I?"

Andrew slid along on the floor like a wounded slug, leaving behind a trail of hot, sticky blood. He dragged himself over towards Dalton who was staring at him wide-eyed, no doubt wondering how the hell she had gotten herself into this situation. Andrew knew how she felt.

Frankie marched forward and kicked Andrew's wounded knee. The pain bloomed again like a nuclear explosion, sending away his vision in a cloud of agony.

"Please," Andrew cried out. "Haven't you done enough? Please, just leave us alone. I'm begging you"

"Why would I do that?" Frankie kicked Andrew again, this time in the side of the head, sending him dizzy. "If I kill the three of you, who's going to say I did anything?"

"The police already have...Andrew's...statements," said Dalton in a half-conscious drawl. We know all about you, Frankie. You'll spend the rest of your life in prison."

Frankie wasn't happy, but it still wasn't enough to deter him. "Well, it still won't do any harm getting rid of the witnesses, will it?" He placed himself down on Bex's bed and she squirmed as he started to stroke her face. "Shall I leave you for last, princess? Let you watch all the fun before I put your lights out?"

"Please," she pleaded. "Just go. Me and my dad won't say anything."

Frankie laughed. "Seriously? You're going to go with that old chestnut? It doesn't work in the movies and I can tell you right now that it doesn't work in real life either, darling."

"Get away from her, you evil bastard."

Frankie looked down at Andrew across the room and laughed. "Or else what, you sad cripple? You couldn't take me with both legs working, so what use are you now?" Frankie put a finger in his mouth and sucked it before holding it in the air. Andrew was forced to watch while he delved it beneath his daughter's blankets.

Bex struggled and squirmed while Frankie cackled almost uncontrollably. His laughter stopped when Rebecca struck his face with her hand. The slapping sound filled the room and was then followed by absolute silence.

Frankie got up off the bed and yelled at her. "Stupid cow!" He lunged forward and punched her in the face. It wasn't hard enough to knock her out cold, but it seemed to knock some of her senses loose, eyes rolling about in her head.

Andrew couldn't help but curse at Frankie, despite the fact it would probably lead to another gunshot. His hatred was too much to contain. "You pathetic cunt! Taking things out on a helpless girl, all because you got passed around jail like a television remote. I bet you've got an arsehole like a clown's pocket."

Frankie pointed the gun at Andrew again, this time his hand was trembling. It was obvious the comments hurt him. But slowly, Frankie got a hold of himself. His hand stopped shaking. He lowered the gun away from Andrew, then pointed it at Bex.

He pulled the trigger.

-31-

Davie got off at the bus stop nearest the hospital. It was only across the road and in less than a minute he was walking through the car park and heading for the main building. He didn't know exactly where inside he would find Andrew or Frankie, but he knew that asking a member of staff would probably be a bad idea. But when he saw the crowd gathering outside the hospital's main entrance, accompanied by a shrill, ringing alarm, Davie knew that finding his brother might possibly be easier than he imagined. Something had happened and it would be a pretty safe bet that Frankie would be involved somehow.

There were hospital employees all over the road comforting patients on gurneys. There were also several police officers standing around grumpily. Davie would have to avoid them all if he had any chance of getting inside the hospital.

He stepped behind a row of cars and made his way forward in a crouch. There didn't seem any possible way to make it through the main entrance without someone stopping him, but there was no other obvious way in. Maybe there was a rear entrance.

He snuck around the back of an ambulance and headed down the side of the hospital. There was a power generator inside a brick enclosure and, beyond that, a wall lined by many square windows. Even further ahead was something that was just what Davie needed: an open fire exit. Only trouble was that a hospital employee was standing there. He was wearing a chef's uniform and puffing on a cigarette as though the ringing alarms were of no concern to him.

"Hey," said Davie, approaching the man nonchalantly. "Having a sneaky fag?"

The man nodded. "I'd just finished my break when the fire alarm went off. Thought it was a good opportunity for another. Managed to buy another pack just as the gift shop was clearing out."

"Won't they be doing a role call or something?"

The man shrugged. "Probably. It's just a false alarm. Do you see any fires?"

Davie shook his head. "In that case, can I go through?"

The man took a drag of his cigarette and blew the smoke in the air. "What is it tonight with people not using the main entrance?"

"What do you mean?"

"Just twenty minutes ago some dude was asking me the same question."

"Really? What did he look like?"

The man narrowed his eyes. "Messed up. Face all ripped up and shit. What's it to you, kid, anyway?"

Davie thought of an answer. "I think it was err...my dad."

The man nodded. "What was he in for?"

Davie continued the lie, seeing no other course of action now he'd started it. "He had an accident at the factory where he worked. That's why his face was injured."

The man took another drag on his cigarette and this time blew the smoke right into Davie's face. "Really? You see that's funny, because he told me he'd been in a car accident."

Davie was stuck for an answer. Making stuff up had never been one of his talents and he'd obviously blown it this time. Before he even had a chance to attempt another bluff the hospital employee had heard enough.

"Just get out of here, kid. I don't know what's going on tonight, but I'm not getting involved. Piss off out of here."

Davie couldn't afford to let the man go back inside and close the door. The hospital was currently deserted and would be the perfect time to reach his brother – if Frankie was indeed inside. It would also be the perfect time for his brother to kill Andrew and his family. Davie had to get through and keep that possibility from happening.

He pulled out the revolver stuffed down his trousers and pointed it at the chef. "Move out the fuckin' way."

The chef looked at Davie and laughed. "You a proper gangster, yeah? What is that, a water pistol?"

Davie laughed back. "Yeah man, I'm a regular OG." He smashed the gun against the man's face and knocked him cold. His body sprawled back into the doorway and Davie wasted no time in stepping over him.

He would have to find his way around the hospital without having a clue where he was going, but there were no other choices. Currently he stood by a cafeteria, but that didn't help much. The hospital had three floors and dozens of departments. It wouldn't be easy to find his brother in this maze. In fact it could turn out to be nigh-impossible.

But when a gunshot rang out, things got a whole lot easier.

The short explosion had come from the same floor that Davie was already on; somewhere down the end of the long corridor in which he now stood. The signs above him pointing in that direction read WARDS 4-7. Davie ran as fast as his battered body could. He was still nowhere near recovered from his car accident, but he tried to put the discomfort aside for now. His trainers squeaked on the floor as he picked up speed.

Davie didn't know what the gunshot meant for certain, but he knew it couldn't be anything good. The odds that someone had just been killed were high and the odds that it was Frankie behind the trigger were even higher.

Either that or the police have just gunned down his crazy brother.

Davie didn't think that was true, though. The police didn't carry guns as far as he knew. They used pepper sprays and batons and stuff. The only time Davie had seen Police with guns was when they shot some nutcase on TV about a year ago. Raul something-or-other. Other than that, the pigs in this country were harmless – nothing like the American cops he watched in the movies. Now they were badass.

Davie reached the end of the corridor and found himself lost again as he faced several options to choose from. He could go left, right or straight on. He chose to stand still and listen, hoping to hear something that would make the decision easier. While he was not absolutely certain, he thought he could hear faint voices coming from a ward on the left: WARD 7.

He headed there immediately and was relieved when he heard the voices again, more clearly. He soon reached a wide, open nurse's station and Davie clearly identified one of the voices as his brother's. What was worrying however, was that all the other voices he could hear were ones of pleading.

Turning a full circle, he tried to hone in on where the voices were coming from. Eventually he settled for a room off to the right. He could not see inside the windows because a curtain was pulled across them, but, as he approached the door, he was certain that was where his brother was.

"Frankie?" he shouted at the closed door.

The voices inside the room stopped abruptly. Then Davie heard his brother's voice reply from inside.

"Davie? Is that you? Get your ass in here, little bro. You're just in time."

-32-

The bullet had hit only centimetres above Bex's head. Andrew's heart had leapt into his throat and stayed there. Now, as he tried to speak, his vocal cords were so restricted that his words came out choked and mumbled. "I can't...b-believe you just...did that. You're insane."

Frankie blew the end of the smoking revolver and then winked at Andrew. "Chill out, yo. I was just making a point, innit?"

Bex had gone the colour of old chalk. The gunshot had been so close to her face that the plaster behind her had fallen away and crumbled into her hair. The smell of cordite filled the room and mingled with the odour of blood.

Frankie strolled over to Andrew and crouched in front of him. "Hopefully I've got your full respect and attention now? I didn't want to have to do that but you gave me no choice, man."

Andrew was feeling weaker by the minute. His mind must have been shutting off to relieve some of the pain pulsing through his kneecap and ribs. "Just... please...enough. Enough."

"Begging again, Andrew? I thought you'd grown bigger balls than that."

"Frankie?"

Everyone in the room looked towards the door. Someone was outside. If Andrew wasn't mistaken, it sounded like Davie.

Frankie edged over to the doorway and leant his head next to the wood. “Davie? Is that you? Get your ass in here, little bro. You’re just in time.”

To Andrew’s surprise, it was indeed Davie who was entering the room cautiously. He’d thought that the boy wanted no part of his brother’s insanity, but the fact that he was here now suggested different. When it came right down to it, they were brothers – they stuck together.

“Little bro, I thought you’d given up on me.”

Davie shook his head. “I was wrong to say what I said. You’re my brother.”

Andrew shook his weary head. I had hope for you, Davie, but it turns out that you’re no better than your brother. To hell with both of you.

A whispered voice snapped him away from his thoughts. He turned his head sideways and saw that Dalton was trying to say something to him. She’d lost every hint of colour from her cheeks now and resembled a ghost more than she did a young woman.

She placed a hand on his forearm. “Grab...my belt. The...canister.”

Andrew tried to figure out what she meant. He looked down at her belt and saw a collection of evenly placed pouches. The one on the furthest-most right contained a small aluminium spray can with a bunch of writing on the side.

Dalton nodded at him. “Grab...it.”

Andrew nodded back, looked at Frankie and saw that he was distracted by a conversation with his brother, then started to creep a hand towards the canister. Inch by inch his fingers stretched towards it, until...

Got it.

He managed to get his hand around the can and started to pull it away from its pouch, but it was stuck on something and would not move. He quickly realised that there was a popper-button attaching a tongue across the top of the can. With his thumb, he unfastened it and started to pull again. The can slid out easily now and his heart beat rapidly as he kept his eyes on Frankie. One false move and the psychopath would shoot him. He would have to keep his movements slow, gradual.

Very, very careful.

Inch by inch.

Frankie turned to face Andrew, eyebrows raised.

Andrew thanked God that he had already managed to slide the canister into the space beneath his armpit.

“What you fuckin’ looking at?” Frankie asked him. “If your eyes were any wider they would fall on the floor.”

Andrew didn't reply. What the hell did Frankie expect him to say? Instead he looked down at the mangled wreck of his knee and thought about the small metal cylinder concealed beneath his armpit and whether he would get the chance to use it.

"So what's your plan?" Davie asked his brother. "You know there's a bunch of police outside, right?"

Frankie shrugged. "The hell they gunna do? Already popped one of 'em. They want to be the ones concerned about me."

"We should get out of here."

Frankie put a hand on Davie's shoulder. "No way, little bro. This is my moment. The day the whole world learns not to fuck with Frankie Walker. The fact that my little brother is here to share it all with me just makes things even more perfect."

Davie looked confused. "Your moment? What are you talking about?"

"Going to whack these bitches, just as soon as everyone comes back in from outside. No point doing it without an audience. Then I'm going to go out in a blaze of glory. Take a few pigs with me if I can. People will remember my name forever. People will have nightmares about me for years."

"You're a fucking psycho," Bex wailed from her bed. Andrew wished she would be quiet, but he assumed at this point it wouldn't make a whole lot of difference. Frankie pointed the gun at her again but this time she didn't flinch. In fact, she seemed more composed and defiant than every.

"Don't be a hater," Frankie told her, "just because you can't understand my greatness. You just don't see the big picture like I do."

Rebecca cackled. It was a cruel sound and Andrew never knew his daughter had such a sound in her. "You think a spree-killing is the big picture? I thought the point of you being here was to get rid of the witnesses, but now you're talking about having an audience. You don't know what you're doing, do you? You're just making it up as you go along, you silly dickhead."

"Plan changed, sweetheart. No shame in it. I figure that if I can't get away with this, I might as well make it count. Gunna go down like a man – a genuine pig-killing hero. You think anyone will ever forget those kids in America that shot up that school? Or that dude last year that blinded that cop? No, they make films about people like that. People will make films about me one day and the whole world will be sorry it ever got in my way."

"Who are you angry at?" Andrew managed to ask from the floor, fighting hard not to pass out.

Surprisingly, Davie seemed to want to know the answer as well. "Yeah. What's this really all about, Frankie? What happened to you?"

"Nothing happened to me, little bro. I'm on top of the world."

Davie shook his head. "No, you're not. You're talking about killing innocent people just so people respect you. When did respect become so important?"

Frankie pointed the gun at Andrew but kept facing his brother dead on. "Respect is the only thing there is. If people don't respect you then you're nothing but their bitch..."

Frankie trailed off slightly and Davie seemed to sense something. "This is all because of what happened in the youth offender's home, isn't it? What the hell did they do to you?"

"He got buggered by the bigger boys," said Andrew, enjoying the sight of Frankie groaning. His face twisted up and he twitched like a madman.

"Shut the hell up, man, or I swear I'm going to make your death so slow it will feel like forever."

"He's right, though, isn't he?" said Davie. "Is that what this is all about? Did someone...hurt you?"

Frankie still held the gun at Andrew, but his arm had begun to shake visibly. "You're chatting shit, little bro. You don't know nothing, so just leave it, okay?"

"I know that this whole situation is messed up," said Davie. "Something happened to you inside that made you lose the plot, big time. Did Andrew have something to do with it?"

"No way," Andrew replied immediately. "I never even met the guy before all this."

Davie shrugged. "So what then? What is it about Andrew that made you go batshit crazy?"

Frankie suddenly turned the gun on his little brother. "I thought you were here to support me, Davie. Stupid me, huh?"

"Support you? This isn't a job interview or a football match. I can't support you murdering people."

"Then get the fuck out."

Davie folded his arms and shook his head. "Not going anywhere. You want me to leave you'll have to shoot me."

Frankie cocked the gun. "Don't think I won't. I'm not afraid to kill anyone. Sick fuckers in the nick learned that shit soon enough. I showed 'em all. Fuckin' nonces."

Davie's ears pricked up. "Who?

Frankie pointed the gun back at Andrew and cocked the hammer. "This fucker!"

Davie looked at Andrew and seemed confused. “Andrew abused you?”

“Yeah,” Frankie said, nodding his head adamantly, tears forming in his eyes.

“What the hell are you talking about,” Andrew cried out. “You’re talking complete nonsense. I never met you before.”

“I don’t buy it,” said Davie. “Andrew doesn’t even work at a prison.”

Frankie’s twitch went into overdrive and a nauseated expression took over his face. “Well...not him exactly. It was McMillan.”

Andrew was stunned. “James McMillan. My half-brother?”

Davie looked at Andrew, obviously confused. “What?”

“My half-brother is called McMillan. I haven’t seen him in years, but his surname is McMillan. Is that who you’re talking about, Frankie?”

Frankie said nothing, but Davie nodded as if something was making sense. “Let me guess, you two look alike?”

Andrew shrugged. “I guess. We have the same eyes and similar hair, but we’re not twins. Like I said, I haven’t seen him in years.”

“You look close enough,” said Frankie, marching towards him and grabbing both sides of his bloodied shirt, yanking him to his feet. “Soon as I seen ya, I thought you was him. Was only when I saw you up close that I realised you weren’t – that that piece of shit must have been your brother or something.”

Andrew shook his head and pleaded. “We haven’t seen each other since I was a teenager. He lived with his father while my mother remarried someone else. He was already ten years old when I was born. I barely knew him.”

Frankie slammed Andrew back against the wall. Pain exploded from his knee. “You share his blood. You probably have the same sick shit running through your veins as he does.”

“I’m sorry,” said Andrew. “I’m sorry for what my brother did to you. I’ll tell the police, make him pay. I promise.”

Frankie released his grip slightly. “You know I actually believe you.”

“Good, because I mean it.”

Frankie nodded. “You know I can’t let you go though, right? It’s too late not to follow this shit through to the end, and there’s no way I’m ever gunna let you tell about what McMillan did to me.”

Andrew grunted. “You killed my wife. There’s no quitting now for either of us.”

He reached for the can under his armpit and pulled it free. His index-finger gripped the release and pressed down hard. A pungent jet of liquid exploded from the can’s nozzle and hit Frankie in the eyes and nose. The excess vapour flew back and entered Andrew's airways as well. Both of them fell to the floor in a choking, spluttering mess.

Andrew's vision was like being under water, all blurs and wet squiggles. His entire face filled with a burning sensation that worsened with every breath he took. While he couldn't see the room clearly, the sound of Frankie cursing was as clear as day. This was it. It would all end now, one way or another.

Andrew placed his palms down on the floor and tried to get to his feet, but it was impossible. The dizziness, twinned with the uselessness of his knee, was too much to overcome. Andrew knew that his daughter was bed ridden and that Officer Dalton was too injured to help. The only person able-bodied enough to help was Davie.

But where did Davie's loyalties lie?

"Come on, man, get up," Andrew heard Davie say to his brother. "We need to get out of here."

"Okay," said Frankie. "You right, little bro."

Andrew sighed. Thank you, thank you. Finally this whole thing is over.

"But I need you to kill them first. Do you still have your gun?"

"No way," said Davie. "I'm not shooting anybody."

"Do. You. Still. Have. Your. Gun?"

"Yes," said Davie. "I have it, but I' not using it."

"Then I'll go down forever, is that what you want? If you get rid of the witnesses then we can sort out some sort of alibi and get through this as brothers. I'll owe you, man – for life. Please, Davie. I need you to do this for me. You're the only person I have."

There was silence in the room as Andrew lay on the floor, terrified and blind, waiting for the next turn of events in this hellish nightmare that had become his life.

"Okay," said Davie. "It's time to put an end to all of this once and for all."

"Thank you, little bro. I love you. You know that, right?"

"I know that, Frankie. I love you, too, and that's the only reason I'm about to do this for you."

There was more silence, interrupted only by what must have been Davie removing a gun he had hidden in his clothing.

"I'm sorry about all this, Andrew," came Davie's voice. "I truly wish none of this had ever happened to you."

Andrew said nothing. He just closed his eyes and replaced the blurriness with darkness. He waited for the end, tried not to listen to his daughter's scream – he didn't want that to be the last thing he ever thought about. So he thought of a time long ago – to the day that Bex was born, back when they had been a happy family. Perhaps in the next life they would be again. He and Pen would still be together.

He listened to the sound of a gun being cocked.

A pause that seemed to go on forever.

Then there was an explosion of sound and the smell of smoke.

Bex wailed.

Andrew opened his eyes.

His vision had cleared a little since closing them, and though he could not make out the finer details, he could see that a body now adorned the floor. A body that was thankfully not his own.

"I'm sorry about your wife," said Davie. "I hope this makes up for it a lit-tle bit."

Andrew stared, trying to understand. He wasn't certain, but it looked like Frankie was lying dead on the floor. Davie had shot his own brother.

Andrew shook his head with disbelief. "W-Why?"

Davie didn't answer the question. Instead, he said, "I'll go and get some help." He dropped the gun on the floor beside his dead brother and left.

Andrew realised that he hadn't taken a breath in almost a minute, and expelled the air from his lungs. Things in the room slowly came into focus and the first thing he made out clearly was Officer Dalton lying on the floor beside him.

"Hey," he said to her. "It's over. Help will be here soon...Officer Dalton...Laura?"

Andrew put a hand on the woman's chest and rocked her gently, and then more firmly. She did not wake up. Her body slid sideways and flopped onto the tiles. The blood had stopped pumping from her stomach and she was no longer breathing. He mourned the loss more than he would have expected. He'd met the policewoman only days earlier, yet she had been a massive part of the reason he and his daughter were still alive. He would never forget what she did for him – Dalton's sacrifice.

"Dad?"

Bex's voice was like music, clearing away the nightmares that filled his head and replacing it with love and hope. She would be safe now, and that made the world bearable again. It was just he and she now, and he would never let anything hurt her ever again.

"Everything is going to be okay now, honey," he told her. "It's over."

Andrew's vision finally cleared and he used it to make certain Frankie was dead. The bullet wound in his temple confirmed it and he gave the biggest sigh of relief that he'd ever taken in his life and then let it out slowly. He was about to lose consciousness, but before he did, he managed a smile.

Yep, he thought sleepily. It's finally over.

Epilogue

April 17th
Dear Diary

Today is my twenty-first birthday. Dad and I spent the afternoon at Mom's grave. We both still miss her every day. Visiting the cemetery helps alleviate some of the pain, but I know it affects Dad differently than it does me. He still blames himself for being unable to protect us that week Frankie forced himself onto our lives.

It still shocks me that Davie Walker shot his older brother that day, to save me and my father. I'll never know the full reasons why he did it, but I can still picture him now, squeezing that trigger as though the weight of the world fought against him. It must have been the hardest thing he'd ever had to do. But he did it anyway. I'll always be grateful to him for that.

After the events in the hospital, the police arrested Davie for murder, but, after they took my Dad's statement about what happened, they offered him a deal: testify against Dom in exchange for a reduced sentence. He was looking at about five years. When my Dad got a lawyer involved, the police dropped the charges altogether. The court case against dad's half-brother, McMillan, is due to start any day now. Apparently Frankie wasn't his only victim; a dozen more have come forward.

Davie went into care after it was discovered what a poor excuse for a mother he had. His identity was withheld to protect him from the media-circus that ensued to cover what came to be known as the West Midland's Massacre. I don't know what happened to him after that, but I hope he's okay.

Eventually my wounds healed and things went back to normal little by lit-tle. We sold the house and moved to the country, away from the pavements and lampposts of urban living, and away from the memories that haunted us. Somehow, I managed to get my head together enough to finish high school and move on to college. I'm at university now – my third year studying Law. All in all, I managed to get through the ordeal Frankie put us through with my mind and body still intact. A scar across my stomach the only physical reminder of the night I nearly died.

Dad hasn't been so lucky. Even five years later, he still walks with a pro-nounced limp. The wounds of his mind are even worse. Sometimes when we watch TV together he starts crying for no reason. His emotions don't work the way they used to. If I go out without calling him every two hours, he panics.

It's not all bad, though. After what happened, there was a media furore about how the police had failed my family, and about how all the red tape in the criminal justice system did nothing but hurt the people that needed protection the most. My dad fronted a campaign to increase police powers, and he succeeded. Now young offenders can be given something called an ASBO and placed on a public register for as long as the police deem neces-sary. They can also be escorted back to their homes if they're caught con-gregating after nine o'clock at night. It isn't much, but It's a start. People have hope again.

After what happened to my dad, neighbourhood watch programs began popping up all over the country and memberships sky-rocketed. People started coming together, fighting back against the thug culture that was threatening to invade our country. If anything good came from my moth-er's death, it's that the UK today is a safer place than it was when she died. Dad holds onto that dearly. Last year he went into politics.

Dad formed an organisation committed to protecting the streets from crime through a series of initiatives. One of those demands the Govern-ment to allocate part of the annual budget to evening activities for impoverished youths. One of the failings that led to much of the UK's gang violence wasteenage boredom. My father helped change all that – he called it Pen's Law. He also spearheaded an investigation into young offender's homes and was disgusted to find out that the claims Frankie made about his half-brother were true.

Officer Dalton was, of course, honoured for dying in the line of duty. No-body, other than her partner, Wardsley,ever knew that she'd let Andrew go after Frankie. Wardsley asked my dad to keep the fact quiet and he'd been happy to. Dalton was a good woman. Once a year we visit her grave; sometimes Wardsley comes with us. I think they were more than just partners.

I guess we'll never know if Frankie was evil or just a result of a crippled and decaying system that failed him from the day he was born. All I know is that the world is a scary place, and that, like my dad, I'm going to do every-thing I can to help make it safer. I don't want any other young girls to lose their mothers the way I did.

This is my last diary entry. At twenty-one I feel I've outgrown the need to analysis my daily thoughts by writing about them. I know myself well enough now. I guess I should end it here. I need to get ready. Dad's taking me out to celebrate my birthday. At least we still have each other...

About The Author

Iain Rob Wright is one of the UK's most successful horror and suspense writers, with novels including the critically acclaimed, THE FINAL WINTER; the disturbing bestseller, ASBO; and the wicked screamfest, THE HOUSEMATES.

His work is currently being adapted for graphic novels, audio books, and foreign audiences. He is an active member of the Horror Writer Association and a massive animal lover.

Check out Iain's official website or add him on Facebook where he would love to meet you.

www.iainrobwright.com
FEAR ON EVERY PAGE

Made in the USA
Columbia, SC
29 December 2018